Antique Shop Mysteries™

Death Takes *a* Holiday

Susan Sleeman

Country Sampler®

CountrySamplerFiction.com

Library of Congress-in-Publication Data
Death Takes a Holiday / by Susan Sleeman
p. cm.
I. Title
                    2016957420

CountrySamplerFiction.com
(800) 282-6643
Antique Shop Mysteries™
Series Creator: Shari Lohner
Series Editors: Janice Tate and Ken Tate
Cover Illustrator: Bonnie Leick

10 11 12 13 14 | Printed in China | 9 8 7 6 5 4 3 2 1

"Are you sure this is safe?" Cringing, Maggie Watson stared up at the rusted motor home parked outside the Carriage House Antiques shop.

"Absolutely." Daisy Carter jingled the keys. "Harry and his buddies take it hunting every year, and they've never had a lick of trouble."

Both members of the Somerset Harbor Historical Society, Daisy and Maggie had become good friends since Maggie had relocated to Somerset Harbor, Maine. Maggie had moved to the quaint coastal town after she'd inherited her late aunt Evelyn's ancestral home, Sedgwick Manor, and the antiques shop located on the grounds. Maggie's husband had passed away a few years ago, and her daughter, Emily, was now in college. It had been the perfect time in Maggie's life to make the move and fulfill her dream of owning an antiques shop.

"We should get going. This snow isn't going to let up on our account," Daisy said. She, Maggie, and Fran Vosburg—a fellow shop owner and member of the historical society—would be making the three-hour drive to Weatherly Village together.

Late-March flurries fell softly around them, but not even the picturesque snowfall could soften the jarring facade of the 1980s motor home. Wide orange paint stripes circled the exterior of the vehicle, and unsightly patches of rust etched the wheel wells—a common side effect of Somerset Harbor's salty ocean air.

"I don't know." Maggie twisted her hands together and wished she hadn't agreed to travel in the decaying tin can—or sleep in it that evening. "Harry's familiar with engines and can fix this monster if it breaks down. None of us knows a thing about car repair."

"Harry assures me it's in fine shape, and you know he wouldn't send us off on a trip if he had any doubts about our safety."

"True," Maggie admitted. "He cherishes you and wouldn't let anything bad happen to you. That's good enough for me. Let's go pick up Fran and get on the road."

The door to the antiques shop opened, and the manager, June McGillis, poked her head out. Snowflakes clung to her short, strawberry-blonde hair as she peered at Maggie. "I'm glad I caught you before you left."

"Is there a problem?" Maggie asked.

"Ruth just called. She said she tried to reach you on your cell, but it went straight to voice mail."

"That's odd. It was working fine earlier." Maggie rummaged in her purse to find her phone. "Oh, I accidentally turned it off. Did Ruth say what she wanted?"

"She wanted to confirm the time we should arrive at Weatherly Village tomorrow."

Ruth planned to drive Ina Linton and June to the village for a promotion that included a two-night stay in Weatherly Manor and the opportunity to dress in period attire for the duration of the long weekend.

"I wish I could be at least half as organized as Ruth is," Daisy said, her tone wistful.

"I'll give her a call once we're on the road," Maggie said. "I have my cell on now, so let me know if you need anything today. Otherwise, I'll see you in the morning." She paused. "Are you sure Nancy can handle the shop for the next couple of days without us?"

"Of course." June grinned. "I trained her, didn't I?"

Maggie returned her smile. "Good point."

Their new temporary employee seemed capable enough, and Maggie needed to trust that she and June had made the right decision in hiring Nancy. Maggie appreciated Nancy's willingness to fill in for them during spring break and to look in on Snickers while Maggie was away. The local high school teacher had assured them that spending a long weekend surrounded by antiques would feel like a vacation to her.

"Come on." Daisy looked up at the dark clouds. "Time to get going."

"See you tomorrow." June waved and then ducked back inside the shop.

Daisy pulled open the motor home's side door, and its hinges groaned. She gestured for Maggie to go first. "After you."

Maggie climbed two tall steps and paused to survey the interior of the home. It was decorated in a vivid orange color that matched the exterior with an added splash of green here and there, and the furnishings appeared worn but clean.

Daisy settled into the driver's seat and gestured at the bucket seat next to it. "Go ahead and sit. When we pick up Fran, the two of you can decide who wants to sit where."

Maggie eased between a pair of orange vinyl captain's chairs to get to the cracked seat. She tried to pull out the seat belt, but it stuck.

"Oh yeah, that thing's temperamental." Daisy wrinkled her nose. "Keep trying and it will come out."

"Will it work in the event of an accident?"

"No one's ever crashed the motor home, so I don't rightly know, but I would assume so." Daisy turned the key in the ignition, and the entire vehicle vibrated as the engine roared to life. "I should have mentioned that Harry souped up the engine."

"Exactly what we need. A rust bucket with extra horsepower." Maggie chuckled. "Is it too late to change my mind?"

Daisy shifted into gear. "Yep. We're on our way."

Maggie finally clicked the buckle into place and peered out the window. The big vehicle creaked and groaned as they drove along the harbor. Daisy's coffee shop, The Busy Bean, came into view, and Maggie felt the corners of her lips turn up at the cheerful sight.

Beneath the shop's yellow-and-white striped awning, colorful chairs sat grouped around bright pink wooden tables, everything deserted in the late-March chill. The shop's logo was emblazoned above the awning—a honeybee dive-bombing a coffee cup. It always brought to mind Daisy's whimsical sense of style. The entire scene was covered with a fresh dusting of snow.

Daisy pulled to a stop in front of Fran's shop, The Quilt Cupboard. The big picture window held colorful bolts of fabric and a large quilt in varying hues of green that Fran had told her was made in the Birds in the Air pattern. Maggie studied the quilt dubiously. She still didn't see any birds in the pattern.

The front door opened and Fran emerged, signaling for them to wait as she spoke with her employee. Slender, almost delicate, Fran wore her dark hair back in a ponytail as usual, her face free of makeup. She wore jeans and a bulky parka with faux fur around the hood.

"It's so hard to leave a business for a long weekend, isn't it?" Maggie asked Daisy.

"Hard, yes, but well worth it to get away from the stress of owning your own place for a few days."

"I can honestly say I've loved every minute of running Carriage House Antiques."

"I love The Busy Bean too," Daisy said. "Most aspects of it, anyway. But when you've managed a business as long as I have, you'll occasionally look for getaways so you can leave it all behind and recharge."

"I suppose so," Maggie said, though she was sure it would be a long time before she felt the need to seek refuge from her beloved shop.

Fran waved good-bye to her employee, then stooped to pick up a purple tote bag and sling it over her shoulder.

Maggie tried to open her door, but it wouldn't budge.

"That thing is finicky." Daisy climbed over the console. "I'll let Fran in on the side."

Daisy opened the door and jumped down. Maggie moved to peer out the side door, standing next to the diminutive kitchen sink that wasn't much bigger than a teakettle.

Fran stared up into the vehicle. "This is Harry's motor home, huh? I hope the inside is in better shape than the outside."

"Not really," Maggie called cheerfully out the door.

Daisy pretended to take offense, her hand coming to her chest, the bright raspberry lacquer on her nails standing out vividly against the lighter pink of her sweater. "I know it's not the Ritz-Carlton, but it's only for one night. I'm sure you'll both survive."

"You're right, it'll be fine." Maggie grinned. "Besides, it will make Weatherly Manor all the more special tomorrow night."

Fran sighed. "I wish I could have signed up for the whole weekend, but I have to get back to the shop by tomorrow afternoon because I'm teaching a class. At least I'll get to sit in on the quilting demonstration in the morning."

"And you'll get to see Lily in her scullery maid role." At the mention of her niece, Daisy smiled fondly. "I love that girl, and it will be so fun to see her all dressed up in historical clothes. Her friend Amanda will be doing the same thing."

"I remember when Amanda worked at The Busy Bean with Lily that one summer," Fran said. "She's a riot."

Daisy frowned. "I wouldn't count on her being so much fun

this time. Lily says Amanda recently broke up with her boyfriend, and she's been kind of moody."

"I have a hard time imagining someone like Amanda letting boyfriend woes get her down," Fran said, "but maybe we can try to raise her spirits."

Daisy ushered her into the motor home. "Let's get going and see."

As she moved aside so Fran could climb in, Maggie picked up a flier for the Weatherly Village Cabin Fever Reliever from the tiny table. The three-day weekend event allowed visitors to stay in the manor house, where they could participate in historical reenactments and craft demonstrations. Pictures of the early-1800s village with a large manor house, a church, stables, barn, and a street of shops decorated the flier.

Maggie was eager to explore the living-history village with her friends from the historical society.

The festivities didn't start until Friday at ten, but Daisy wanted to be there first thing in the morning to see Lily.

Fran approached the table and tapped the flier. "I really wish I could spend Friday and Saturday night with you all." She sighed. "Dressing up in period costume sounds like so much fun."

"We wish you could too," Maggie replied.

"Make sure you take pictures of everyone all dressed up." Fran slid her finger down the flier to the activities list. "Maybe you and James can take a sleigh ride. If you do, I want to see pictures of that too."

James Bennett, Somerset Harbor alderman, historic preservation consultant, and Maggie's good friend, would arrive tomorrow as well. Although he wasn't a regular member of the historical society, he was always available to lend a hand, and he had said he was very interested in the architecture of the buildings in the reenactment village. His love of history was something he and Maggie shared.

Daisy clasped her hands. "Oh *yes*. A romantic sleigh ride for the two of you would be perfect."

Maggie rolled her eyes good-naturedly and changed the subject. "Where should we sit so you can get this thing on the road? Do you want the passenger seat, Fran?"

"Go ahead and take it. I brought some fabric along to cut quilt squares and I'll have more room to do that in the back."

Maggie resumed her place and wrestled with the seat belt again.

Daisy slid behind the wheel, and her lips tipped up in mischief. "Don't think that was the end of my nudging you toward a sleigh ride."

Maggie clicked her seat belt in place and gave a resigned sigh. "I didn't think it would be."

Daisy fired up the engine, startling an elderly man who was plodding by on the sidewalk. He glared up at them, and Maggie offered an apologetic wave. He merely responded with a shake of his head and walked on.

Daisy drove along the harbor, where the ocean crashed against the wharf. They passed the majestic white Somerset Harbor Lighthouse, which was set on a rugged cliff. The historical society had recently bought the picturesque monument in an effort to preserve the town's most distinctive landmark.

As Daisy merged onto the coastal highway heading north, Maggie looked out the window to see the shoulder fall away steeply to craggy rocks and the ocean waves pummeling the Maine shoreline below. It was beautiful in a fierce kind of way. She had nearly driven off this road once, and she held a healthy respect for it.

She glanced at Daisy. "You *have* driven this thing before, right?"

"Tons of times." Daisy waved a dismissive hand.

"Still, would you mind keeping both hands on the wheel and both eyes on the road?" Fran asked as she spread out her fabric swatches on the seat next to her.

They all laughed, but Maggie offered a quick prayer that they would reach their destination safely. She kept her own eyes on the road until they left the seaside behind and made their way inland. Though average temperatures at this time of year were in the midforties, a recent spring blizzard had left high snowbanks lining the road, and temperatures had been hovering at the freezing mark for the last few weeks.

Maggie turned her attention to the flier. "Other than seeing Lily and the quilting demonstration, what do the two of you plan to do at the village?"

"You mean besides making sure you get in that sleigh with James?" Daisy winked.

"Daisy Carter, if you plan to keep this up all weekend, you can stop and let me out." Maggie wagged a finger at her irrepressible friend.

"Okay, okay. I'll back off." Daisy grinned, and Maggie knew "backing off" meant Daisy would only bring it up daily instead of hourly.

"I won't have much time, but I really want to take a horse-drawn snow roller ride," Fran said. "I've read about snow rollers in history books, but I've never seen one in action."

"I'd never even heard of them before I saw this flier." Maggie flipped through the brochure and studied the picture of a heavy wooden drum that was about six feet in diameter being drawn by a team of horses. The roller had been used in the nineteenth century to compact the snow on roads to make passage easier for horse-drawn sleighs.

"I'm going to the cooking demonstration at the farmer's cottage," Daisy said. "And I'll be joining the rest of you for the cooking demonstration with the manor house cook too." She shook her head, her teased-up bun tottering with the movement. "I know that seeing all of the work women went through in the good old days will make my daily chores at The Busy Bean seem so much easier."

"What about you, Maggie?" Fran asked.

"I'll be admiring all of the local vendors' antiques with June and maybe purchasing some nice authentic pieces for the Carriage House."

"And?" Daisy prompted.

"And I look forward to meeting Jasmine and Lily. Amanda too," Maggie answered stubbornly, to spite Daisy's fixation on her taking a sleigh ride with James. Jasmine was Daisy's sister and Lily's mother.

Daisy thumped her palm on the steering wheel. "I keep forgetting that you're the only person in the group who hasn't met my family."

"Not yet. But I love how Jasmine kept up your family tradition of using a flower name for her daughter."

Daisy chuckled. "Lily, on the other hand, isn't so thrilled about it."

"She's seventeen," Fran said. "She's not supposed to be happy about anything but boys."

Maggie swiveled to look at Fran and grinned. "This coming from the only woman in the group who is young enough to remember what it's like to be that age."

"Right, because being over forty makes you so ancient," Fran teased.

"It doesn't, but when one has a daughter about the same age as Lily, the teenage years sometimes seem a lifetime away."

"Speaking of Emily, how's she doing at school?" Daisy asked.

Maggie launched into talk of her sweet daughter, and the miles quickly slid by. By the time they turned off the highway onto a snow-packed road, the sun was minutes from setting.

"According to the map, the village is three miles ahead on the right," Daisy said.

Fran looked up from her fabric. "I was surprised to hear the village is open year round."

"Yep," Daisy answered. "The board of trustees has done an amazing job of planning events all year long to keep revenue high enough for repair and upkeep of the property. Plus, it's a bonus for kids today—shoot, even old people like us—to have a living example of how pioneers survived Maine winters."

"There." Maggie pointed ahead at a rustic road sign for Weatherly Village. "I wonder what would have happened to this property if the family hadn't insisted on the estate being preserved."

"We'd likely see the ruins of the house, or a new house in its place." Daisy braked, and the motor home fishtailed.

Maggie clutched the armrest and held her breath until the vehicle righted itself.

Not fazed at all by the skid, Daisy clicked on her blinker and turned onto a road even narrower than the one they'd just traveled. Tall eastern white pines lined both sides of the road, obliterating the last bit of the day's sunlight and casting the motor home into the eerie shadows of twilight.

Maggie shuddered.

"You sure you can handle this weekend, Maggie?" Daisy asked. "You're shivering, and we haven't even gone outside yet."

"We will have heat in here tonight, right?" Maggie asked.

Daisy laughed. "Don't you know by now that I take good care of my guests?"

The motor home bumped over the rutted drive, and Maggie prayed that the monstrous vehicle would make it safely down the road in the waning light.

She caught sight of a light burning bright at the entrance to the village and glanced down at the map they'd received with their registration packet. "The parking lot is to the left about a quarter of a mile ahead."

The lot was filled with several cars. All of them were covered with an inch of snow except a blue minivan that had its headlights on.

"That's Jasmine's car," Daisy said as they drove past. "She's always on time."

Maggie grinned. "So you and your sister are nothing alike, then."

Daisy looked indignant. "I can be on time if I want to."

"You just never want to," Fran said.

"Exactly."

By the time Daisy parked in a designated RV space, Jasmine had climbed out of her van. She quickly picked her way through undisturbed snow, pulled open the motor home's side door, and climbed the stairs.

"About time you girls got here," she said, her eyes sparkling as she loosened the colorful scarf around her neck. "Welcome to the village."

Where Daisy was a brunette with bright blue eyes, Jasmine had thick red hair, which fell softly to her shoulders in waves. Her green eyes sparkled above freckled cheeks.

"Ladies, this is my sister, Jasmine. Jazzy takes after my mom," Daisy said preemptively. "In personality as well as looks. She's got Mom's fiery personality, while I'm like our dad—even-tempered and easygoing."

Fran and Maggie shared a dubious look. Maggie extended her hand to Jasmine in greeting. "I'm Maggie Watson."

Jasmine shook Maggie's hand. "Daisy's told me all about you and your adventures in solving mysteries."

Maggie laughed. Naturally that had been the information Daisy had chosen to share. "That's me. A real Sherlock Holmes."

"Or *Watson*," Daisy joked. "Either way, our little town is far more exciting now that you've moved there."

"I'll second that," Fran added and smiled at Jasmine. "Good to see you again, Jasmine."

"You too." Jasmine looked around the space. "I thought all the ladies were coming. Lily's going to be disappointed that she won't get to see the whole gang."

"Don't worry." Daisy swiveled her chair around. "Everyone is driving up tomorrow morning. Except Liz. She has church responsibilities."

"That's understandable. She is the pastor's wife." Jasmine glanced at her watch. "It's almost time for our tour."

"Do I have time to get the water and electricity hooked up before it's pitch-black outside?"

Jasmine nudged her sister. "With my help you do."

"I'd help too," Maggie said, "but I have no idea what to do."

"Me too," Fran said.

"No worries." Daisy stood. "I'll grab a flashlight and pliers, and Jazzy and I will be ready to go in no time."

"I have to see this. Who knew Daisy had a rustic side?" Maggie grabbed her coat and hat and twisted a scarf around her neck, Fran doing the same beside her.

They all tromped down the stairs behind Jasmine.

"Mom!" A frantic cry cut through the air. "Aunt Daisy!"

Maggie turned to see a teenager sprinting toward them. Her hair was as red as Jasmine's, but it lacked her mother's soft waves. Her round face was ghostly pale, and her green eyes were wide with fear.

Jasmine hurried to meet her daughter. "What's wrong, Lily?"

"It's Amanda. She was supposed to meet me at the car for a ride home, but she didn't show up. No one's seen her for ages. This is so unlike her, and I'm really worried."

"Did you try calling her?" Jasmine asked.

"I did, but she's not answering. I texted her too. No

response. I think something bad has happened to her."

Jasmine patted Lily's shoulder. "Don't worry, honey. You've only been off work for an hour or so. She could have gotten a ride with someone else."

"But she disappeared before that. One of the girls in her training group said they all left the manor house at four o'clock to go over to the dressmaker's shop to pick out their costumes. When they got outside the manor, Amanda realized she'd forgotten her mittens and ran back for them. They went on to the dressmaker's shop without her." Lily's chin trembled. "Amanda never showed up for her fitting, and she knew she'd need her costume for tomorrow. She'd never flake on that."

"Did you ask anyone else about her?" Maggie asked.

"As many people as I could, and then I remembered you all would be here soon. I thought you'd help, so I came to find you."

"So, the last place anyone saw Amanda was at the manor house around four this afternoon," Maggie said. "That means she's been missing for about two hours, correct?"

"Yeah. I called her mom . . . you know, to see if she had to leave early but forgot to tell me. But her mom thought she was riding home with me." The shaking in Lily's hands increased. "We have to find her. She's not wearing a heavy coat or boots, and it's freezing out here."

"And it looks like you're cold too," Jasmine said. "Let's go inside where you can warm up, and we can sort this out together."

"No, Mom, we have to *do* something."

"We will, honey, but we need to know everything about the day first. It will make our search far more productive." Jasmine wrapped an arm around Lily and led her to the door.

Daisy faced Maggie. "I have a bad feeling about this. If Amanda started walking only two hours ago, there's no way she could make it to the nearest town before dark."

Maggie considered the possibilities. "I hope for her sake that she left with someone else."

"But who?"

Maggie stared across the snow-blanketed area, the dark settling in and deepening the ominous shadows. "That's what we need to find out."

2

Following Daisy's instructions, Maggie helped her connect the electricity and water to the motor home quickly, and then they headed inside, where Daisy started the heater running. Clearly distressed, Lily sat in one of the captain's chairs, fidgeting with the fringe on her scarf.

Jasmine knelt next to Lily and rested a hand on her daughter's knee. "Now. Tell us about the last time you saw Amanda."

Maggie quietly slipped off her jacket and settled into a nearby chair.

"I saw her at lunch. Our training sessions were held where we're assigned to work this weekend." Lily shifted her focus to Maggie. "Amanda and I both play scullery maids. She's working at the manor house, and I'm at the inn."

"And you saw her at lunch?" Maggie asked.

"Yeah. All of the staff had lunch together in the community hall."

"And did anything seem odd about Amanda?"

"No . . . I mean, yeah . . . maybe. She was really distracted."

"Then she could have missed hearing where and when to meet you," Jasmine suggested.

"No, she heard. I made her repeat it." Lily looked at her mother. "Like you do when you don't think I'm listening. I got in her face and said, 'Parking lot at five thirty. Be there.'"

"What happened after lunch?" Maggie asked.

"We went back to training. My group got out at a quarter after five. Her group was already dismissed and heading for the gate. I ran to catch up to them, but she wasn't with them. I thought she'd probably run ahead to have a . . ." Lily glanced

19

nervously at her mom. "Amanda started smoking, Mom. Don't get all worked up, okay? I don't smoke. It's gross." She turned back to Maggie. "So I thought she was going to have a cigarette because I don't let her smoke in the car."

"But she wasn't at the car," Maggie prompted.

"No, so I called her. Then texted. She didn't respond, so I freaked a little bit and ran over to the other workers in her group to ask about her. That's when they told me about her forgetting her mittens." Lily sighed. "I can't shake the feeling that something bad has happened to her."

Jasmine squeezed Lily's hands. "It's okay. We'll find her."

"Try calling her again," Daisy suggested.

Lily got out her phone. "No signal. It's kind of iffy around here. Sometimes you get one, sometimes you don't."

"Maybe it's your carrier."

"No," Lily said adamantly. "I've borrowed phones from people who have different carriers. Everyone's signal is hit or miss in this area."

"Then perhaps Amanda hasn't returned the calls or texts because she didn't receive them," Daisy said.

"I thought of that, but . . ." Lily frowned. "My gut still says something's wrong. Like I said, she knew she had to get her costume for tomorrow, and she wouldn't miss that. Besides, where would she go? We're in the boonies out here, and she's not an outdoorsy person. She wore a hoodie today instead of her jacket because she said it matched her hat and mittens. She'd never try to hike out of here, especially dressed like that. She had to have left with someone in a vehicle."

"Can you think of who that might be?" Fran asked.

Lily pursed her lips and glanced at her mom.

"Don't worry, honey," Jasmine said. "Whatever it is, you can tell us. We all want to help."

"It's Kyle. Kyle Jensen."

"Amanda's old boyfriend?" Jasmine asked.

"That's the one." Lily looked at Maggie and Fran. "He works here too. He's really mean and controlling. He's hurt her before. Nothing bad enough to send her to the doctor, but he's bruised her arms."

Jasmine sucked in a breath.

Lily's gaze cut to her mother. "I'm sorry, Mom. I wanted to tell you, but Amanda made me promise not to."

"I'm glad you told me now," Jasmine said, clearly troubled by the delayed revelation.

Maggie could sympathize with Jasmine's concern. As a mother, she wanted to believe her daughter felt secure enough in their relationship to confide in her, especially if a friend was in trouble.

"And she stayed with him after that?"

"Yeah, I told her it wasn't a good idea, but she . . ."

"Loves him?" Maggie prompted.

"She did then. Or at least she thought she did."

Maggie nodded. "But they're not together anymore."

"Kyle graduated last year, and he keeps getting fired from his jobs 'cause he does drugs," Lily explained.

Jasmine pulled in another sharp breath.

"Don't worry, Mom. Amanda doesn't do drugs and neither do I. We know better than that. Amanda wouldn't put up with him taking drugs, so she broke up with him two months ago."

Maggie saw Jasmine's shoulders relax a notch. With a teenage daughter of her own, Maggie could well put herself in Jasmine's shoes. Maggie knew the pitfalls a teenager faced these days. She was so grateful that Emily had made wise choices in life and was doing well in college.

Maggie reached into her tote bag for a notebook and pen and wrote down Kyle's name. "Has Amanda seen Kyle since they broke up?"

"All the time. He shows up wherever we are and kinda stares at her. It's really creepy," Lily said. "We even saw him today. He signed up to do this job before Amanda dumped him. She asked him not to do it, but he didn't listen. He's a farmhand here. It cracked us up to think he was scooping up horse . . . well, you know. Their stuff."

She flashed a weak smile, but it disappeared as quickly as it came. "He bugged her at lunch today. Like all up in her face. She couldn't even eat. I told him to leave her alone, and he finally did. Amanda tried to eat, but she seemed to lose her appetite after that. I suspect she was thinking about yesterday. I sure was anyway."

"What happened yesterday?" Jasmine asked.

"Kyle got really mean. Looked like maybe he was hungover or having withdrawals or something, and he cornered Amanda. He said if she wouldn't be with him, she wouldn't be with anyone else. He'd kill her or any guy she started seeing."

"Why didn't you tell me?" Jasmine demanded.

Lily shrugged. "It's not like we thought he'd do anything for real. But now . . ." Her voice faltered, and she bit her lower lip.

Now he may have taken Amanda, Maggie thought. "Is there any possibility that they reconciled and she went somewhere with Kyle voluntarily?"

"No," Lily said. "No way."

"Maybe we should call the sheriff," Daisy suggested.

"Yes. But first, let's check in with whoever's in charge of the training," Maggie said. "They might know something we don't. Or did you already do that, Lily?"

"No, I haven't."

"Then we should go see this person right now."

"That would be Mr. Radcliff. He's the manager and has an office in the town square." Lily jumped up and zipped her jacket. "I can take you there."

She rushed to the door, and they all quickly donned their outerwear and followed her. Outside, the snowfall had tapered to light flurries, and the moon shone brightly. Maggie looked up to see clearing skies and shining stars, but that meant the temperature was dropping fast, and if Amanda had somehow gotten lost on the large property, they needed to find her soon.

Maggie wound her scarf around her neck and hurried ahead of the group to catch up to Lily, who was just crossing a slippery wooden bridge. Maggie grabbed the handrail to steady herself, but Lily powered over the slats with the fearlessness of youth.

Near a ticket booth and turnstile, Lily swiped a card through an electronic reader at the gate. When the gate popped open, she held it for the others to enter. When she let go, the metal clinked closed, and they entered Weatherly Village.

Maggie couldn't help but be awed by the sight of the quaint village unfolding before her. She felt as if she'd been transported to the past, and she longed to stroll through the town and take in each historic detail—once they'd found Amanda safe and sound. For now she would settle for catching glimpses of the charming little hamlet as they passed under the glowing gaslights that illuminated their path and the fluttering snowflakes. Lily moved over the brick sidewalk at a brisk clip, leading them past a small church with a white steeple. Next they passed a one-room schoolhouse painted a vivid red.

Walking deeper into the village, Maggie saw the charming shops that lined Main Street. Black wrought-iron signs with gold lettering hung over each doorway. They passed the milliner, the cobbler, the bank, and a cozy inn.

The last building on their side of the street had a sign that read Board of Selectmen, which was another name for the town council. A light shone through the window of the building, and Maggie glanced inside to see a middle-aged man sitting at a desk. His full head of black curls was so thick it resembled a cap. Lily opened the door, and the bell above tinkled. The man watched them as the group filed in, the dark circles under his eyes pronounced in the dim light.

They entered a room with wide pine floors, white walls, and a primitive oak desk.

"I suppose you all are here for your tour," the man said as he stood. He was dressed in plaid trousers and a white shirt with wide cuffs, over which he wore a silver brocade vest and a bow tie.

Maggie introduced each member of the group, then added, "I think the tour will have to wait."

The man introduced himself as Donald Radcliff and fired a mistrustful look at Maggie. "What's this about delaying the tour?"

"Do you know where Amanda Caldwell is?" Lily blurted.

He looked startled for a moment, then furrowed his brows. "I was told all the workers had departed for the day."

"It seems as if Amanda was last seen in the manor house around four o'clock," Maggie said. "And she didn't meet Lily at her car at five thirty as they had planned."

"Oh dear," he replied, his expression deadpan. "What do you think has happened to her?"

"We were hoping you might know."

"Me? No no. Like I said, I was told that everyone had gone. If I'd known a young girl was missing, I'd have made sure someone was looking for her."

Maggie relayed the information Lily had shared about Kyle.

"I see," Mr. Radcliff said. "I guess I'm not surprised about Kyle. I had reservations about him from the start."

"Then why hire him?" Daisy asked.

"It's difficult to get young men to work out here. Not many of them are interested in history these days. They want sports or video games. Even fewer are willing to do honest work like mucking out stalls. They'd rather put on sloppy pants that hang to their knees and listen to obnoxious music."

Though Maggie didn't quite agree with his assessment of modern young men, she knew the conversation would go more smoothly if she avoided arguing with the man. She nodded polite understanding. "Would you allow us to see if Kyle is still here?"

A sour look spread over Mr. Radcliff's face. "I suppose we could go down to the barn to check."

"That would be wonderful." Maggie squeezed Lily's arm, but the girl seemed lost in her thoughts. Maggie suspected there was something else that Lily wasn't telling them, but asking in front of Mr. Radcliff likely wouldn't elicit a helpful response, so Maggie decided to wait until she could speak to Lily alone.

He picked up a black wool Coburn greatcoat and slipped into it before pressing a bowler hat on his head. The hat bobbed up as if it couldn't contain all of his hair, and he pressed it down harder. He looked a bit irritated by the garments, and after grabbing a modern-day flashlight from his top drawer, he led them out of the office. Outside, he used a modern key and deadbolt to secure the door.

As if feeling Maggie's eyes on him, he turned to her. "We like to keep things as authentic as possible, but with today's world we do use current locks to keep out thieves. Especially at the manor house, where our most valuable antiques are kept. Every item in the home is certified—no reproductions—and the pieces are not only valuable in terms of money but are priceless heirlooms of the Weatherly estate."

He traipsed ahead, his booted feet sinking into the fresh snow and creating a trench through the white powder that glistened in the beam of his flashlight.

He rounded a corner where the brick sidewalk ended, then crossed a road to the crest of a hill that sloped away over the wintry landscape. "I'm afraid this is as far as our gaslights go. You'll want to stay close to me."

Without the warm lights, the village felt dark and foreboding, and Maggie didn't have to be told twice to move close to him. The group huddled together, and they soon stopped in front of a large white barn.

"No lights on," he announced. "I doubt anyone is inside."

He ran his flashlight beam over the area, revealing several sets of footprints in the snow. They overlapped and ran in circles as if several people had played in the snow.

Maggie eyed them. *Signs of a struggle?*

The prints trailed off toward the barn. Mr. Radcliff walked closer to the building, his light coming to an abrupt halt as it passed over something on the ground. Maggie caught up to him and spotted bright red-and-purple knitted items poking up from the snow.

"Mittens?" Maggie asked.

Lily broke free from her mother and squatted next to Maggie. "They're Amanda's mittens."

"Don't touch them," Maggie warned.

Lily looked up at Maggie, her eyes wide with unease. "But if they're here . . . if she . . ."

Maggie gave Jasmine a pointed look. "Maybe it's time to take Lily to the motor home."

Jasmine nodded and reached out to help her daughter stand.

Lily pulled away and firmed her chin, reminding Maggie of Daisy. "Amanda's my friend. I'm not going anywhere."

Maggie could see there would be no changing the girl's mind. She caught Daisy's eye. "I think it's time to call the sheriff."

3

Maggie and the others stood watching Deputy Matthews as he stepped in and out of nearby buildings to check for any signs that Amanda had been there. Short and stout, he wore a navy blue hat and uniform that included a warm jacket. When he returned to the area where Amanda's mittens had been found, he squatted down.

He mumbled something Maggie couldn't make out, then came to his feet and focused on Lily. "You're sure these mittens belong to your friend?"

"I'm positive," she replied. "Her grandma knitted them for her. They're one of a kind."

The deputy turned his attention to Mr. Radcliff. "Is there any other way off the property by car besides the main drive?"

"The only other way out at this time of year is on a sleigh, snowshoes, or a snowmobile."

Deputy Matthews shined his flashlight over the area. "No tracks of any kind except footprints here and leading to the main exit. I suppose the recent snow could have buried other prints." He peered at Lily. "Might Amanda have taken a hike?"

"Amanda? No way. She would never go for a hike, especially not in the winter. She hates the cold."

"Our property is over four hundred acres," Mr. Radcliff added. "A lot of it is wooded, so we always warn the staff in training not to wander."

Maggie feared that meant Amanda was indeed in trouble, and she offered a quick prayer for the young girl's safety.

"That's right," Lily added. "It was one of the first things they told us."

Daisy moved closer to the deputy. "Please tell me there's something you can do to find her."

"You can be sure we'll do our very best and assign resources as needed. I'll get with dispatch right away, and we'll put out an alert and cover all the obvious routes out of the area." He faced Lily. "How recent is the picture you showed me on your phone?"

"It's from yesterday."

"Okay, good." He reached into his pocket and withdrew a business card to hand to Lily. "Text it to my cell, and I'll get it to dispatch. I'd like Amanda's cell number as well."

Lily held out her phone. "No signal here. I'll move around until I find one."

"Could I get one of your cards too?" Maggie asked when Lily walked away.

He flashed her a questioning look but dug into his pocket and handed her the card. They all stood in silence until Lily returned.

"I sent the text," she said. "You should receive it as soon as you get a signal."

Deputy Matthews fished a notepad and pen from his other pocket. "Can you describe what Amanda was wearing today and give me more details about her physical appearance?"

"She's about five foot eight. She has brown eyes and blonde hair, and she weighs maybe 140 pounds. She had on skinny jeans, a red sweater, and a white hoodie. Her boots are tan suede. She also has a hat that matches the mittens. She loves vintage video games and was wearing silver Pac-Man and Ghost earrings. She has a small butterfly tattoo on the inside of her wrist. She just got it and doesn't want her mom to know, so she wears a white watch to cover it up. Oh, and she's eighteen, if that matters. Is that enough?"

"Enough? If we had even a quarter of this information for most missing-persons cases, the investigations would be solved a whole lot faster." He attempted a smile but was met with only somber expressions. "I'll need to go to my car to file a report and dispatch deputies to look for Amanda. I'd like to do it immediately, but I'll need you all to promise not to come any closer to the mittens than you are now. Not only might the evidence be tainted, but we need to be careful not to create any more footprints for us to analyze. Time is of the essence. If my sergeant determines it's necessary, I'll cordon off the area when I finish with dispatch, but I'd like to get the alert out ASAP."

"So you think something bad has happened to her?" Lily asked.

"I didn't say that. She may have voluntarily left with another person, but I want to be proactive."

"We really appreciate it." Maggie gave the efficient deputy a grateful smile. "Will you also contact Amanda's parents?"

"Yes. Now if you don't have any other questions, I'll get moving."

"Please don't let us keep you," Daisy said.

He tromped away through the snow.

Maggie faced the others. "There's nothing more we can do out here."

"And it would do all of us good to eat dinner," Daisy added.

"Eat?" Lily's voice shot up and rang through the quiet. "How can we eat?"

"Because we know we have to keep up our strength if we're going to help find Amanda." Jasmine took Lily's arm and led her toward the village's main gate.

Maggie fell into step beside Mr. Radcliff. "I suppose you'll need to stay at the village until the deputy finishes up for the night."

"Yes, I will." He frowned. "I can't imagine having this area cordoned off with that awful yellow crime scene tape you see on the news. Especially not on such a big weekend. The Cabin Fever Reliever is our main winter event with all the vendors."

Maggie hadn't been thinking of the weekend's festivities at all, but she supposed she could see where Mr. Radcliff would be concerned. He did have a job to do, but she thought it seemed rather callous that he was more troubled over the weekend's potential losses than the whereabouts of one of his employees.

"I'm assuming a detective will be assigned to this case. Perhaps you can ask for him or her to come out early in the morning so by the time you open, the investigation will be finished and the tape removed."

"Yes . . . yes, I suppose that will have to do." He gestured at the road. "I'll walk out and talk to the deputy at his car."

Maggie strode down the street past shops that were dark and shut up for the night, and she longed for daylight. Not so she could see inside the shops or get a better look at the entire village—although she looked forward to that too—but so that the light of day might bring with it news that Amanda had shown up at home safe and sound.

They walked in silence, and as they passed the church, Maggie offered another prayer for Amanda. They soon reached the bridge, where small icicles had formed on the handrail. She slid her hands along the metal as she walked to keep from falling, dislodging the icicles. Some dropped into the creek and floated away, while others hit dry land and broke with a tinkle.

On the far side of the bridge, Mr. Radcliff turned toward her. Before he could bid her good night, she made a beeline for the patrol car. Deputy Matthews sat behind the wheel, his radio at his mouth. He held up a finger as she approached and continued his conversation. When he finished, he climbed out and settled his hat on his head.

"You really do have a problem getting cell signals out here," he said to Mr. Radcliff.

"It's hit or miss. In fact, we had to call you from my office landline."

"At least I have my radio."

"Will a detective be sent out to investigate the incident?" Maggie asked.

"If Amanda is still missing in the morning and we have reason to believe foul play is involved, a detective will be assigned."

Maggie dug out her business card and offered it to him. "Will you have the detective call me?"

He took it but gave her a quizzical look. "If you don't mind me asking, what exactly is your role in all of this?"

"Lily has asked us to help find Amanda. I'm a friend of her aunt's and just want to do my part."

He arched a brow. She could tell he wanted to say something, but he held his tongue.

"Will you be going back to the area where we found Amanda's mittens?" she asked.

"I'll take a more thorough look, snap a few photos, and collect the mittens as evidence. Not much more I can do in the dark."

"And what about blocking off the area with that awful yellow tape you see on television?" Mr. Radcliff wore an expression of intense disgust. "You won't need to do that, will you?"

"If I find something else in my inspection that warrants protecting the scene, I will have it cordoned off. If not, then no."

Mr. Radcliff frowned, drawing down an already long face. "You know, it would be very bad for business if visitors were given the impression that a crime had taken place here."

"I understand, Mr. Radcliff, but I will do whatever I think is necessary to find this young lady."

"Certainly." He readjusted his hat.

Maggie felt sorry for the manager. He was in a difficult position with the weekend's events scheduled to start in less than twenty-four hours, but Amanda's well-being had to come first. Maggie was beginning to question why he didn't see that.

She bid both men good night and crossed the parking lot to the motor home. Inside, she reveled in the warmth from the heater and took off her jacket. Daisy and Fran stood in the miniscule kitchen making grilled cheese sandwiches and heating a pot of tomato soup.

Daisy flipped a gooey sandwich and then looked up. "Good timing. The sandwiches are almost ready and so is the soup. I made it at The Busy Bean this morning."

Maggie loved Daisy's cooking, but she couldn't gather up much enthusiasm for food at the moment. "Thank you, Daisy. Soup is the perfect thing to eat on such a cold day."

Maggie's gaze went to Lily, who was slumped in a booth seat at the small dining table. She held her phone and was staring at the screen. Jasmine sat next to her, her hands clasped tightly in her lap.

Maggie hated to ask Lily additional questions when she was so worried about her friend, but she couldn't dodge the feeling that Lily was leaving something out. If they were going to help find Amanda, Lily needed to share all of the facts, however difficult it might be.

Maggie hung her coat on one of the captain's chairs and slid into the booth facing Lily. "Would you mind if I ask you a few more questions before we eat?"

She didn't look up. "Go ahead."

"Is there anything else about Amanda that you might not have mentioned?" Maggie asked gently.

Lily gnawed on her lower lip and continued to stare at her phone. Jasmine opened her mouth to speak, but Maggie held up a hand to stop her. If Lily didn't realize she had to tell them everything, she might not be completely truthful, and that wouldn't bode well for Amanda.

The three of them sat silently as time ticked by, the only sound the sizzling of butter when Daisy flipped a sandwich.

"I think she was seeing another guy," Lily finally said, her voice not much more than a whisper. "Someone who works here."

"But you don't know for sure?" Maggie asked.

Lily shrugged forlornly. "She wouldn't say. But this whole week when we came out here for training, she'd have moments when she got all dreamy."

"Maybe it was Kyle," Jasmine suggested. "Sure, he was abusive, but maybe she was thinking about getting back together with him. She didn't tell you because she knew you wouldn't approve."

"That's not possible!" Lily burst out, slamming her phone on the table. Contrition filled her eyes when she looked up to see her mother's shocked expression. "Sorry, Mom. I didn't mean to yell, but Amanda was totally over him."

"Okay, so maybe there *is* another guy," Maggie said. "But you're her best friend. Why wouldn't she tell you about him?"

Lily stared over Maggie's shoulder. "I think the guy might be too old for her. Or worse. He could be married."

Jasmine gasped, drawing Lily's attention. She sat silently watching her mother as if waiting for a rebuke.

"What makes you think that?" Jasmine asked softly.

"Some things she said." Lily shrugged again. "I could be wrong though. That's why I didn't say anything. That, and I thought you'd be mad, Mom."

Jasmine took Lily's hand. "I don't like hearing all of these things about Amanda, but I'm glad to hear you're thinking clearly and not going down the same path. And I'm proud of you for not only doing the right thing, but for telling us about Amanda when I know you want to be loyal to her and not share."

"I wouldn't have said anything if I didn't think it would help find her." Lily looked at Maggie. "So does this help?"

"Did you mention this to the deputy?"

"I didn't. I don't know anything for sure so . . ."

"He needs to know. If he's not still outside, I'll try to call him. Is that all right with you?"

Lily nodded.

"I'll check to see if he's here." Maggie stood. "And then I'm going to go straight to Mr. Radcliff and get a list of employees so we can review the names and you can tell me as much about the male employees as you can."

Lily chewed on the inside of her mouth. "I don't really know a lot of them."

"But you can probably point out the ones who are kind of cute, right? The kind of guys that Amanda might be attracted to?" Maggie smiled.

A tiny grin flickered on Lily's face. "Yeah, maybe."

"Then that's where we'll start." Maggie grabbed her coat and held out her hand. "If you'll give me your key card so I can get into the village, I'll try to get that list from Mr. Radcliff."

Lily dug her card from her pocket and handed it to Maggie. Maggie turned and found Daisy standing with her back to the cooktop and her hands planted on her hips. She was giving her best "Where do you think you're going?" look.

"You're going to see him right now?" Daisy asked. "Dinner's ready."

"I don't want to waste any time. Can I take a sandwich to eat on the way?"

Daisy wrapped a sandwich in wax paper. "I don't like the thought of you out there alone. One of us should go with you."

Maggie didn't want to drag any of them away from their meal. "I'm guessing Mr. Radcliff and the deputy are still here, and I should be fine. Just save me some soup. It smells amazing."

"You got it."

Maggie chomped into the sandwich and savored every bite of the gooey cheese on thick sourdough bread as she headed for the village entrance. The snow had completely stopped, and the temperature had dropped a few more degrees. The thought of sitting inside, toasty warm with a hot bowl of soup in front of her, made her footsteps falter for a moment.

She had to hold onto that thought as she hurried through the brisk wind blowing snow over her feet. She saw that the deputy's car was gone, which she took to mean that he hadn't found any other evidence. She quickened her pace, hoping Mr. Radcliff hadn't gone home too. She kept her head down and munched on the sandwich as her mind flew over the possible reasons for Amanda's disappearance.

Lily had mentioned that Amanda didn't like hiking or the cold, so Maggie didn't believe she'd wandered off into the woods of her own volition, but that didn't mean that the girl hadn't put herself in harm's way. Teenagers often acted on a whim, and with Amanda already rebelling in many ways, she could very well have taken off with another guy and neglected to tell anyone.

Maggie shoved the empty wax paper into her pocket and picked up her speed. She found Mr. Radcliff exiting his office. "Mr. Radcliff."

He spun and raised an eyebrow as if to say, "What now?"

"I was wondering if you could give me a list of the village employees."

"I can't do that. Confidentiality rules prohibit me from doing so."

"I don't want to put you in an awkward position. All I want is their names in case Amanda is with one of them."

"Madam, this is not your concern. I've given the authorities all the information they need, and they're the ones who will be following up on this."

"I understand. I'll check with Lily again and see if she can think of any names of people Amanda might have been seeing."

Maggie paused. "I'm sure you want to get to the bottom of this as soon as possible, and I hope I'll be able to help."

"You're right. I do want to get to the bottom of this." He looked away from her and gestured for her to start walking toward the main entrance of the village.

She complied. "I imagine it's quite a job keeping up with all of your employees."

"Especially the ones in lower positions. Maid and farmhand jobs tend to have a high turnover rate. As I mentioned earlier, the young people today aren't very interested in history or putting in a hard day's work."

Maggie peered down the picturesque street. "I would have loved to work in a charming village like this when I was younger, but I can see where it would be a struggle to keep the village staffed."

"That's why I try to be good to the staff we have. Like providing lunch during training. And yet a lot of our younger workers take it for granted. I don't have to provide lunch, but I read in a book on business that mealtimes are good opportunities for the workers to get to know each other and bond."

"Have you noticed Amanda bonding with anyone in particular?"

"It seemed like there was always some guy or another hanging around her table." He frowned. "She was a bit of a flirt."

"That didn't affect her work, did it?"

"Not that her trainer has told me." He yawned, and Maggie was reminded of the lateness of the hour. She wanted to take advantage of her time alone with Mr. Radcliff to gather information, so she pressed on.

"If Amanda isn't found by morning, would you be willing to show me the areas that she frequented today?"

He hesitated. "The village opens at ten, so the latest I could do it is at nine. Does that work for you? Otherwise, you'll have to show yourself around."

"Yes, thank you very much," she replied. She hoped that when morning came, investigating Amanda's disappearance would no longer be necessary. Her heart clenched at the thought of what it could mean if Amanda was still missing by then.

4

As the sun climbed into the sky and filtered through the faded curtains of the motor home, Maggie dressed quietly to keep from waking the others. Anxiously waiting for word on Amanda, they'd all stayed up late the previous night and finally crashed around two o'clock. Everyone, especially Lily, needed to sleep, and they were all still resting peacefully. Maggie could have used a few more hours of sleep too, but she wanted to get a good look at the area where they'd found Amanda's mittens before the staff arrived and destroyed any evidence the deputy might have missed in the dark.

She slipped on her jacket and patted the pocket to make sure Lily's key card was still inside.

Daisy opened one eye and raised her head from her pillow groggily. "Where are you going so early?"

Maggie crept closer to the bed that had been converted from the RV's little dining table. In a whispered tone to keep from waking the others, she explained her intent. "Go back to sleep. I'm sure I'll be back in time to cook breakfast."

"I could come with you."

Maggie put a hand on her friend's shoulder. "Jasmine and Lily will need you when they wake up."

"You're right." A frown marred Daisy's usually bright countenance as she propped herself on her elbow. "I hate that my precious niece has to go through this. She's been looking forward to this weekend for so long. Since she's so worried about Amanda, Lily might not want to play her part as scullery maid." Daisy sighed. "Lily loves history, and this would have been so exciting for her."

"It sounds to me like she inherited your love of history, and I'm sure she has your tenacity too. Why else would a seventeen-year-old spend her spring break working here?" Maggie patted Daisy's hand. "I'm sure she'll pull through this ordeal just fine. Plus, Amanda could turn up any minute, and then Lily can continue to enjoy her time here."

"Sure," Daisy agreed, but it was halfhearted.

"You know, unless the deputy starts a search party, there's not much Lily can do for Amanda," Maggie said. "Maybe you should suggest she carry on with her maid's position to keep her mind busy."

"You could be right. I'll suggest it."

"Now go back to sleep."

Daisy smiled, an earnest one that lifted Maggie's spirits as she went outside and drew in a quick breath of the chilly morning air. Fortunately, no additional snow had fallen during the night, leaving the blanket of whiteness undisturbed save for the footprints and tire tracks crisscrossing the area. Presumably, the lack of fresh powder would make it far easier to ascertain if Amanda had been spirited away on a snowmobile.

An old sedan sat in the parking lot, the snow brushed from the vehicle. Had Mr. Radcliff arrived at work already, or was it someone else? Maggie surmised that it couldn't be someone up to no good, since they surely wouldn't announce their presence by parking so close to the motor home.

Maggie took a moment to dial Ruth's number and was relieved when the call went through. She told her about Amanda so that James and the other historical society members would be up to speed when they arrived. Maggie also reminded Ruth about the welcome lunch scheduled for the group at the manor house that day.

Confident her friends would offer their support to Jasmine and Lily when they arrived, Maggie set off, keeping her eyes open for snowmobile, snowshoe, or sleigh tracks. She spotted nothing except car tire tracks leading back to the main road.

She crossed the bridge and slipped through the turnstile, then took a moment to admire the area. At the first bend in the winding road, the small white chapel stood against the backdrop of a snowy scene that wouldn't have been out of place on a postcard. Maggie imagined what it would have looked like in the early nineteenth century: the pathway leading up to the church lined with parishioners in their gowns and formal suits, the doors flung open, and the minister standing in his black garb to greet them.

She continued on, fighting the urge to stop at the red one-room schoolhouse as well. Main Street was as picturesque as she'd imagined last night. Each shop was painted in different colors from the era, and several had bright canvas awnings mounted over the doors. She stopped outside the darkened window of Mr. Radcliff's office, puzzled. *The car in the parking lot must belong to an employee, but who would arrive so early?*

She turned the corner, where a sharp wind caught her by surprise. She put her head down and huddled deeper into her jacket. Her breath came in little puffs. Though it was frigid now, today's high temperature was supposed to hit forty degrees. The snow would melt on the roads and sidewalks, making it much more comfortable for visitors.

She turned to take in the rest of the village and caught her first view of the manor house high on a hill overlooking the town. A traditional two-story colonial, it was painted a cheerful yellow and had a wide porch that wrapped around the house. Three chimneys stood tall on the black shingled roof, smoke puffing from one of them. Maggie noted small footprints leading away and up the hill toward the manor house. She suspected they belonged to a woman. Perhaps the owner of the car in the lot had started a fire in one of the home's many fireplaces.

She trudged down the hill and away from the manor, past the small caretaker's cottage, where larger footprints cut a path from the home toward the livery stable. Maggie supposed that the live-in caretaker could have gotten up early to prepare for the day's festivities. *Or perhaps the footprints are from last night, around the time Amanda went missing . . .*

She continued on to the barn. Deputy Matthews hadn't strung the yellow tape as Mr. Radcliff had feared, but the mittens were gone, taken into evidence. She moved closer and made a grid search, covering every inch of the area. Nearer the barn, she spotted a few dark spots in the snow. She removed her gloves, squatted next to them, and gently brushed the snow away from the spots to reveal dark red drops of what appeared to be blood.

Her heart sank. *Please don't let this be Amanda's blood.*

Maggie pushed aside more of the snow and found more splotches of the stuff. The more she uncovered, the more convinced she became that the substance could only be blood. She whisked her fingers over the area and found additional footprints overlapping one another.

Had there really been a struggle? It seemed possible, and the thought that she could be destroying valuable evidence made her stay her hand. She snapped pictures with her cell phone and then got to her feet. She dug out the deputy's card and dialed. There was no signal, so she headed back up the hill until two bars appeared on her screen. She dialed his number again. The call went to voice mail, and she left an urgent message for him to return her call.

Pondering her next move, she surveyed her surroundings. Smoke was still curling up from the manor house, and she considered checking out the person who'd made the tracks leading up to it, but she couldn't think of a good reason to do so. Her best bet was to return to the motor home and wait for the deputy to call or for Mr. Radcliff to arrive so she could ask him to protect the area from foot traffic.

She hurried down Main Street to the motor home and found everyone up and dressed.

Lily was folding a blanket, and her face lit up when she saw Maggie. "Did you hear anything about Amanda?"

"Not yet. I'm sorry. I'm sure we will soon, though."

Lily looked crestfallen, and Maggie desperately wanted to help the young woman. On her way back, Maggie had warred over telling them about the blood she'd found, but with Lily's reaction just now, Maggie decided to keep it to herself until after she'd spoken to the deputy. After all, the blood could be from an animal or an injured worker, and she didn't have the authority or the know-how to jump to conclusions about her discovery. Worrying Lily wouldn't help her cope with her friend's disappearance. Maggie decided to stay positive for the sake of Daisy's niece.

"So what's everyone planning to do this morning?" she asked to lighten the mood.

"Lily decided to keep her scullery maid role." Daisy took a frying pan from a small drying rack. "And Jasmine and I will take turns hanging out at the inn with her."

"I'm so glad you decided to go on with your role," Maggie told Lily.

"Mom says Amanda would want me to do that, so I am. But I'm also going to talk to everyone on staff who might know something about her."

"I'd appreciate it if you would let me be the first to talk to the guy you mentioned might be dating Amanda. I would rather not give him a chance to fabricate his story or come up with an alibi if he knows something about her disappearance."

"Okay, if that's what you want, but I'm gonna ask everyone else about her." Lily's jaw was set with determination.

"Please do, and if you learn anything, please let us know right away." Maggie turned to Daisy. "I'm dying to try cooking on that petite stove, so I'd like to make breakfast."

"Who am I to stand in your way?" Daisy handed the frying pan to Maggie. "Have at it."

Maggie cooked scrambled eggs and sausage, the delicious aroma of sizzling sausage soon permeating the small space. Fran cut up a cantaloupe, and Daisy toasted English muffins while Jasmine chatted with Lily at the table.

Daisy pushed half of an English muffin into the toaster. "I sure hope Lily's going to be okay," she said under her breath.

"If only Amanda would show up," Fran said, her tone wistful.

Daisy moved closer and kept her voice low. "Jasmine got a call from Amanda's mother this morning. She wants to come out here, but she's out of the country on business and having a hard time finding a flight home on such short notice. I feel terrible for her, but Jazzy said she seemed to be holding up well enough. I don't think anyone wants to consider that Amanda might not be missing by choice."

Fran's forehead creased. "My heart breaks for her, and Lily too."

"We'll find Amanda," Maggie said, injecting confidence into her voice that she didn't feel, especially after finding the blood that morning.

She continued her quest to remain upbeat through the meal, and as they were finishing up, the deputy phoned.

"Thank goodness the call got through," she said.

Maggie moved toward the door for privacy. Outside, the signal strength grew even stronger. "Is there any word on Amanda?"

"No, sorry," the deputy replied. "But I understand you may have some information for me?"

"I may have found something that can help." Though she'd already told him in her message about her discovery, she recounted it for him again. "Once I saw the blood and prints, I moved away before I contaminated any evidence."

"Detective Brad Adams is on his way," Deputy Matthews said, but he didn't comment on the evidence she'd uncovered. "Would you be willing to meet him and show him what you found?"

"Absolutely."

"I'm not sure when the village workers start arriving, but could you also station yourself near the area to keep anyone from disturbing it?"

"I'll head over there right now." She confirmed that he'd given her cell number to the detective in case he needed her, and then she disconnected the call to go inside and tell the others of her plan.

"You can use my key card again," Lily said. "But we'll need it to get inside later."

"Maggie, why don't I walk you to the gate and let you in? Then we'll hang on to Lily's card," Daisy suggested.

Maggie agreed and started for the door again. Fran hurried after her.

"Can I go with you?" Fran whispered. "I think Lily needs some time alone with her mom and aunt."

"I'm always glad for your company."

"Let me grab my jacket."

Maggie waited for her to slip into her coat, and then opened the door in time to see Mr. Radcliff pull into a nearby parking spot and climb out of his car.

"Daisy, you can stay here if you want. Mr. Radcliff can let us in." Maggie nudged Lily, trying to brighten her mood. "I'm really looking forward to seeing you in costume."

"Thank you." A hint of a smile graced Lily's lips.

Maggie and Fran crossed the parking lot to Mr. Radcliff. Dressed in the same coat, hat, and trousers as last night, and with the same dark circles hanging under his eyes, Mr. Radcliff bore the telltale signs of having spent a very troubled night.

She greeted him and quickly brought him up to speed on Amanda's situation.

"I guess we'll have that crime scene tape after all," he grumbled.

Maggie resisted the temptation to remark on the fact that there were far bigger problems than the aesthetics of the village, and instead explained Deputy Matthews's plan. "Would you mind if we wait for the detective inside?"

"Follow me." He marched toward the turnstiles and slid his card through the reader, motioning for Fran and Maggie to lead the way through.

Maggie set off at a quick pace, but Fran fell behind.

"Oh my," she said, stopping near the church. "Isn't this a lovely sight?"

"Picturesque for sure. I'd love to see the inside."

"It will be open at ten with everything else," Mr. Radcliff said. "And we have a Sunday service you can attend."

"Unfortunately, I have to leave after the quilting demonstration this morning," Fran said dejectedly.

"You could stop for a quick look on the way out of the village," Maggie suggested.

"Good idea." She peered at Maggie. "But now we should get going, right?"

Maggie appreciated that her friend understood the sense of urgency. When they reached the barn, she was also thankful to see the caretaker hadn't trampled through the area. She had expected Mr. Radcliff to join them, but he didn't even peek around the corner from his office.

Near the blood spatter, she came to a halt and turned to Fran. "Do you find it odd that Mr. Radcliff seems more concerned about the business than about Amanda?"

"Now that you mention it, yes. Do you think he could have something to do with her disappearance?"

"I don't have any reason to believe he's involved, but he does seem entirely consumed by running this business and little else."

"If that's the case, I would think he's a very difficult man to work with. There's so much more to life than making money."

"Spoken like a woman who knows how to run a business *and* keep her priorities straight. Maybe we're being too hard on him. Perhaps the board of directors is putting pressure on him."

"It sure sounds possible." Fran shivered.

"You don't have to stand out here with me," Maggie said. "I'm sure Mr. Radcliff would let you sit in his office until the quilting demonstration starts."

"I'm glad to keep you company, and it also gives me a chance to study these amazing buildings." Fran held her hand over her eyes to block the sun as she turned in a circle. She came to a stop facing in the direction of the manor house. "Please remember to take lots of pictures so I can share in your weekend experience."

"I will," Maggie promised. "And I'm sure Daisy will have stories to tell. Especially if—*when*—Amanda is found safe and sound."

Hearing footsteps, they turned to see a husky man over six feet tall striding down the hill. He was dressed in civilian clothes and had dark, close-cropped hair and deep brown eyes that fixed on them with great intensity.

"Ms. Watson?" He stuck out his hand.

"Yes, I'm Maggie." She took his hand and stifled a wince at his strong grip.

"Detective Brad Adams," he said, shifting his focus to Fran. "And you are?"

Maggie introduced Fran and told him everything she'd learned so far, ending with her morning discovery. "There's very little of it, but it does appear to be blood."

"Can you show me where you found it?"

"Of course."

"I'll wait here," Fran said.

Maggie led him to the splotches. He crouched down for a closer look. "Not enough to indicate a serious injury. Still, I'll collect a sample."

"And what about the footprints? I thought it looked like a struggle had occurred."

"Honestly, Ms. Watson, these could be from a single incident or from people walking over the snow in both directions."

"True, but—"

"I'll poke around some more, and if I believe we need to cast the prints, then we'll do so."

"Okay, good," Maggie replied, though he was acting a little too laid-back for her liking. "Do you have any other questions for me?"

"Not at the moment." He stood. "Don't worry. I've been a detective for ten years now and have a good closure rate on my cases. I'll find Amanda. You can be sure of that."

She glanced at her watch to discover it was nearly time for her appointment with Mr. Radcliff.

"I should tell you the cell reception here is spotty, so if you do have any other questions, I'm staying at the manor house this weekend, and you should be able to find me around the village."

"Thank you for your help, Ms. Watson."

She returned to Fran. "I asked Mr. Radcliff for a tour of the areas where Amanda was spotted yesterday. Would you like to tag along?"

Fran pushed up her sleeve to look at her watch. "Sure, but don't let me get so caught up that I forget to go to the quilting demonstration."

"I'll do my best."

Together, they climbed the hill, but when they reached Mr. Radcliff's office, the lights were out and the door was locked.

"What do you make of that?" Fran asked.

"We're early, and I get the impression that he's a very punctual person. He's probably doing some last-minute inspections around the village."

"Why don't we do some window shopping while we wait?" Fran suggested. "The cobbler shop next door looks interesting."

"Good idea."

They strolled to the store with historically accurate shoes of all sizes displayed in the window.

"Do you think your Weatherly Manor costume will include shoes like these?" Fran asked.

"I hadn't thought of that." Maggie cringed. "I remember reading that shoes in this era were made on straight lasts, and they don't distinguish between the right and left feet. I can't imagine how uncomfortable that would be."

"Victorian-era ladies were made of sterner stuff, I guess."

Maggie gestured inside, where the cobbler sat with his back to them, stoking a cast-iron stove for heat. "The cobbler's here, so why don't we ask if we can look around?"

"Sure."

Maggie opened the door. The small shop smelled of leather and shoe polish and had original hardwood floors. A large wooden workbench lined the far wall with an assortment of tools hanging above. Maggie spotted a curved awl, a chisel-like knife, and a cobbler's hammer lying on the workbench. There was no sewing machine in the shop, since they hadn't been used in shoemaking until the mid-1800s. Until that time, cobblers had made shoes by hand for centuries. She appreciated the staff's attention to detail and commitment to historic accuracy.

The cobbler turned. He had snow-white hair and spectacles

worn low on his nose. Maggie pegged him to be in his eighties. He was a slight and stooped man. His pants were tucked into tall boots, and a tattered leather apron covered his white shirt. She could easily picture him sitting down at the workbench and hammering away at shoes.

"We aren't open for another hour or so," he said, but his voice was kind and his smile was warm, accentuating the laugh lines that ran over the leathery skin at the corners of his eyes.

Maggie took an instant liking to him. "We have some time to kill. We're early for a tour with Mr. Radcliff. Would it be okay to look around?"

"Sure," he said. "You must be VIPs if Donald is giving you a tour."

"Not VIPs exactly," she replied. "I'm Maggie Watson and this is Fran Vosburg. We're friends of Lily Grainger, and we're trying to help locate her friend, Amanda Caldwell."

"Frederick Ingerson," he said, holding out a callused hand to each of them. "And as you can see, I'm the cobbler." His grandfatherly eyes narrowed. "I heard that poor girl went missing. I wish I could help, but I don't know her."

Maggie got out her cell phone and showed him Amanda's picture.

"Oh yes. I remember seeing her around." He closed the stove door.

Maggie stowed her phone. "Maybe you noticed something yesterday that you didn't think was important. Around four in the afternoon, which is when she was last seen."

"Hmm." He tapped his chin. "Something odd did happen, but it was near the end of our shifts."

"Oh?" Maggie prompted.

"The man I share rides with works in the livery. He was a bit late, so I went to find him and ran into him at the corner. I was turning back when I saw this new farmhand hurrying toward the barn. I remembered him from lunch yesterday. He's kind of a brash young man, and I'd heard Donald Radcliff scolding the kid for not listening during his training. I think Donald called him Carl or Lyle."

"Kyle?" Fran asked.

"Yes. That's it. Kyle stormed toward the barn, and I could tell that he was mad. Then he started arguing with another person."

"Do you know who with?" Maggie asked, trying to hold back her concern upon hearing that Kyle had been bickering with some unknown person near where Amanda's mittens had been found.

"Sorry, but no. They were in the shadows, and it was too dark to tell if it was a man or woman, but I recognized this Kyle fellow's voice from the other day when he threatened a young woman at lunch, saying something about if he couldn't have her, no one could. Made quite a scene."

Fran frowned. "That was Amanda he threatened. The girl who disappeared."

"That's not good then, is it?" Frederick asked. "I wish I had heard more of the argument, but all I could make out was Kyle saying, 'You're going to pay.' Then he must have lowered his voice or the argument ended, because I couldn't hear anything else."

"Do you think he could have been talking to Amanda? A woman's voice wouldn't carry as well as a man's," Maggie said.

"I don't know. It could be that."

"What about your friend?" Fran asked. "Did he see or hear the person Kyle was harassing?"

Frederick shook his head. "We both listened carefully, and in fact, we thought about going down there, but you know, I'm not so young anymore, and this Kyle kid is a big strapping fella. I didn't want to risk getting mixed up in a personal matter, but now . . . oh, goodness . . . now, with Amanda missing, I wish I would have stepped in."

Maggie wished he had too. Amanda's situation seemed to grow more ominous by the minute.

God, she prayed, *please keep her safe and let us find her soon.*

5

"I need to talk to Kyle right after I meet with Mr. Radcliff," Maggie said as she and Fran opened the door to the manager's office at exactly nine o'clock.

He looked up and offered them what he must have thought passed for a smile, but it actually looked more like a grimace. "You're here for the tour, I suppose. Where would you like to begin?"

"I'd like to visit any of the locations Amanda might have been yesterday."

He stood. "That would be the manor house and the community hall, where group training and lunch were held."

"And where was she supposed to be fitted for her costume?" Maggie asked.

Slipping on his coat, he joined her by the front window. "Costumes are made and altered by the dressmaker in her shop right over there." He pointed across the street at a purple building with a needle and thread etched on its large glass window.

Maggie noticed a trio of workers strolling down the street and seeming out of place in their casual modern attire. She looked at Mr. Radcliff. "You came dressed in your costume, but the other workers are in street clothes."

"We don't like to have the costumes leave the property. We have volunteers who launder and mend them on site. As manager, I'm an exception," he added, as if the special treatment was his due.

"Where do the staff members keep their personal possessions?" Fran asked.

"Each building has a designated place to store and lock up personal belongings. If a costume gets soiled or damaged, the employee must fill out a request form and turn the clothing in to the dressmaker."

Maggie assumed it took a large number of volunteers to keep all of the costumes clean and in good repair.

"I imagine the men who work in the barn turn in the most requests," Fran said.

"Actually, in the heat of summer, the women's gowns trap heat and need to be cleaned more often. And don't get me started on how they drag on the ground and collect all manner of disgusting things." He shuddered with obvious distaste, then suddenly froze, his gaze fixed on something outside.

"What is it?" Maggie asked.

He gestured to a young man walking down the street. "That's Kyle Jensen. His shift doesn't start for thirty minutes, and trust me when I say he never comes to work early. Just getting here on time is a huge accomplishment for him."

More interested than ever in Kyle after the cobbler's story, Maggie observed his progress down the street. He was around six feet tall with broad shoulders and sandy brown hair in a buzz cut. He was carrying tan overalls and a blue striped shirt. Maggie imagined that a man of his size and build could easily overpower Amanda, and her insides grew cold at the thought. "Is that his costume he's carrying?"

"Yes, and from the direction he's coming from, he had to have taken it home with him last night." Mr. Radcliff crossed his arms. "That's an infraction, and it's going to go on his record."

Kyle strode up to the dressmaker's shop.

Fran moved closer to the window. "What do you think he's doing?"

"I guess he's leaving his costume for cleaning or mending."

As if he'd gotten into a fight and tore it or got blood on it?

"Can we go check?" Maggie tried to hide her concern, but it rang through her voice.

"Absolutely. I need to discuss this with him anyway." Mr. Radcliff held the door for them and locked the deadbolt behind them.

Maggie hung back. She wanted to watch Kyle's reaction while Mr. Radcliff confronted him. She and Fran trailed after Mr. Radcliff across the street and soon found themselves blinking in the dimness of the dressmaker's shop.

The walls were lined with bolts of fabric and small drawers with hand-lettered labels like Buttons, Bows, and Lace. Maggie admired the lovely nineteenth-century iron chandelier bedecked with porcelain flowers hanging above. A petite woman in a gingham dress and white bonnet stood behind the counter. Maggie wandered over to marvel at the antique sewing items on display, especially a Tunbridge Ware cotton barrel much like one Maggie had seen at an auction. Bands of painted colors circled the little wooden barrel. She gently unscrewed the top to see a small spool of cream thread, the end peeking out through the tiny hole in the side.

Kyle stood at the counter, talking and gesturing agitatedly to the dressmaker as she frowned down at Kyle's overalls.

Maggie wanted desperately to toss questions at him, but she warned herself to play it cool so she didn't come on too strong and spook him.

"I can't have these ready by your shift today," the dressmaker was saying. "Blood is tricky to get out."

Maggie sucked in a breath and heard Fran do the same. *Blood?*

Abandoning her promise to stay calm, she rushed toward the counter. "I need to talk to you, Kyle."

He turned to glare at her, displaying raw red scratches running down the side of his face.

A sick feeling about the origins of those scratches slithered through the pit of Maggie's stomach, but she swallowed hard and forced herself to maintain eye contact.

Kyle eyed her in return. "Who are you?"

"Someone who's trying to find out what you did to Amanda."

"Amanda?" His eyes narrowed. "What's wrong with Amanda?"

Maggie planted a hand on her hip. "You have to know she went missing last night."

His mouth fell open in an almost comical look of stunned disbelief, but Maggie assumed he was playacting.

"I live in a small town and know how fast news circulates," she said. "You must have heard about this."

He shrugged. "I was home playing video games all night. Didn't talk to anyone."

"Was anyone home with you?" she asked, taking the opportunity he presented to check his alibi for the evening hours.

"My mom." He looked away as he spoke.

Most people can't look you in the eye when they lie to you. She resolved to contact his mother to confirm his alibi. "Those are pretty nasty scratches on your face, and that's an awful lot of blood on your clothes. How did that happen?"

"Wait." He shot her a pained look as his fingers drifted to his cheek. "You think Amanda did this? No way. I'd never hurt her. I love her."

"Then how did you get scratched?"

He didn't answer. He simply stood fidgeting and avoiding eye contact.

She didn't know what to make of his mixed signals. On the one hand, he really seemed to care about Amanda. On the other hand, he seemed nervous, and Maggie was certain he was lying—or at least hiding something.

Mr. Radcliff stepped forward. "I'd like an answer to that myself."

Kyle blew out a breath. "I got scratched when I was pruning the raspberry patch out behind the barn."

Maggie didn't know a lot about gardening, but she suspected caring for any plant when the ground was still frozen and covered in a blanket of snow was not common practice. "Odd time of year to prune berry bushes."

He eyed Mr. Radcliff. "If I want to keep my job here, I do whatever I'm told to do."

"You want to keep working here?" Mr. Radcliff asked incredulously. "You certainly haven't been acting like it."

"Yeah, sure. I'd stay on after this weekend. It's a cool place."

"You're a history buff, then?" Maggie asked.

He flashed a look of annoyance before he controlled it. "I like learning about the interesting stuff, yeah."

He was lying again, but why? Maggie scrutinized him, and he avoided her gaze.

"You wouldn't want to stay here so you could keep an eye on Amanda, would you?" Fran offered in a soft voice.

"Why would I do that? We broke up."

"From what I've heard, you're not happy about that and want to get back together," Maggie said.

He shrugged again and tugged up the waistband of his sagging jeans.

"In fact," Maggie continued, "I just learned that you argued with someone outside the barn around five thirty last night."

He crossed his arms but didn't speak.

"Is that true?" Mr. Radcliff demanded.

"No."

Mr. Radcliff's gaze didn't waver. "Then why would people say you were?"

"'Cause they're out to get me, I guess."

"Why would anyone be out to get you?" Maggie asked.

"Depends on who they are. I'm a fine-looking guy with everything going for me, so I'm bound to have made someone jealous. It was that way all through high school. Why would it change now?"

Maggie decided not to respond to his comment. She didn't think there was anything she could say that the overconfident young man would believe. She decided to get straight to the point. "Amanda's mittens were found in the area where you were seen. Were you arguing with her?"

Her words had the desired effect. All the fire went out of his eyes, to be replaced by a cold emptiness. "Get it through your head, lady. I didn't hurt Amanda. I love her, and now I'm more worried about her than you are."

"Then tell me the truth about the argument so I can find her."

"I don't know how it's any of your business." He shifted his gaze again.

One minute his sincerity for Amanda seemed believable and heartfelt, but the next he was evasive and standoffish. The only thing she was certain of was that he didn't plan to tell her the truth about his whereabouts the night before.

"Since Amanda's mittens were found in the area where you were seen arguing, I advise you to think about telling the truth. If not to me, then to the police when they ask."

He firmed his jaw and stared her down.

"And the blood on your costume," Mr. Radcliff said. "How'd that happen?"

"The raspberries. I got scratched and bled on my costume."

She faced Mr. Radcliff. "I think we should have a look at the raspberry patch."

Maggie saw Kyle swallow hard, but he didn't speak.

"I'll escort you over there myself," Mr. Radcliff replied. He directed a stern look at Kyle. "See that you get new clothes and get to your station by the time the village opens."

"That's why I came in so early."

Right. Maggie didn't buy his reason for coming in before shift. She thought it most likely that he came in early not out of a sense of responsibility, but to hide the damage to his clothes. And he might have come in to try to cover up additional evidence as well.

She stopped Mr. Radcliff before he could leave the shop. "Can you make sure the blood isn't touched on this costume until Detective Adams has had it analyzed?"

He studied the costume on the counter for a moment before barking orders to the dressmaker. "Set the costume aside until I clear you to launder it."

She nodded, her eyes wide. Maggie felt a twinge of pity at the unsettled look on the poor woman's face.

"Have a nice day," Maggie said to her by way of apology and followed Mr. Radcliff outside, where they were caught up in a throng of workers making their way toward their respective buildings. Their casual attire brought to mind another place she should visit.

She caught up to Mr. Radcliff. "Will you also show me where Kyle would have stored his costume?"

"Look, this is a very busy weekend for us. I have a business to run here. I can't be showing you around all day long, you know."

Fran checked her watch and piped up in the stunned silence that followed. "I'd like to get a front-row seat for the quilting demonstration, so I think I'll go find the building."

"That will be the community hall," Mr. Radcliff said. "I might as well show you the way and take Ms. Watson to the barn while I'm at it."

Without a word, he turned off of Main Street and started down the hill toward the old white barn. They passed Detective Adams, who was busy rolling out crime scene tape.

Mr. Radcliff paused. "Kyle's storage area is in the barn, but the community hall is a little farther along this road. Since your friend has to go there for the quilting demonstration, why don't we do that first and double back?"

"Thank you for thinking of me," Fran said.

He nodded curtly and marched ahead of them.

Maggie and Fran shared a look.

"He's hard to read, isn't he?" Fran asked under her breath as they followed him down the hill.

Maggie shot an amused glance at Mr. Radcliff's back. "He's a bit of a curmudgeon. On the bright side, though, except for a few grumbles and general reluctance, he's been mostly cooperative."

Once they had reached the community hall and Fran had disappeared inside for the quilting demonstration, Maggie turned to Mr. Radcliff, who was starting to look impatient. "Tell me about training and lunch yesterday."

"This room was set up with ten tables and chairs surrounding them," he said. "The front of the room held tables with our catered meals. We had a group meeting in the morning before the workers went to their assigned buildings for training, after which they returned here for lunch." He took a breath as he hit his stride, clearly at ease in a position of authority. "Our staff is educated not only on the history behind their Weatherly Village professions and the appropriate nineteenth-century etiquette, but also on current customer-service techniques and cash handling."

"That makes a lot of sense," Maggie said. "How did Kyle do in customer-service training?"

"He wasn't what I would call a raving success like Amanda and Lily were." He frowned. "It takes a lot of time and effort to train our staff. I hope when Amanda is found that she and Lily will want to continue working here on weekends. I think they're going to do very well with the customers."

Again Maggie was struck by the fact that he seemed more concerned about the success of the business than his employees' well-being.

"Do you like your job, Mr. Radcliff?" she asked.

"Of course." He looked startled by the question.

"Are you under a lot of pressure from the board for financial success?"

"Pressure? No. Why do you ask?"

"You seem more focused on the business than . . . anything else," she said, softening her comment by not expressly mentioning Amanda.

He stared at her for a long moment, apparently deep in thought. "You mean I don't appear worried about Amanda. I can see where you'd think that, but I am. And not only for how it might affect the business." He sounded as if he were trying to convince himself as much as Maggie, and her unease deepened.

"Can we move on to where Kyle stored his things?"

He turned on his heel as if eager to leave and strode toward the barn, where Detective Adams had finished stringing the dreaded tape. Maggie stopped and told the detective about Kyle and the bloody costume. "The dressmaker is holding off on getting that stain out if you need to test the blood."

"Thank you again, Ms. Watson. I appreciate your willingness to help."

"I'm glad I can be of assistance. I know if it were my daughter out there, I would want anyone and everyone to do their part to find her."

She watched Mr. Radcliff walk toward the barn and took a moment to study the exterior. She noticed that there were two levels to the building: one built into the hillside, the second accessed by a rise in the ground level. Mr. Radcliff had entered the upper level through a large sliding door. The smell of hay filtered out, and she saw that the haymow took up the entire upper floor.

"Do you keep cows on the property?" she asked.

"We only keep oxen for pulling our demonstration plows. They winter inside on the lower level, which was once used as the milking parlor." Mr. Radcliff entered the haymow and crossed to a cupboard in the corner. From his coat pocket, he fished out his ring of keys and unlocked the door.

Maggie searched through the cupboard but found nothing more than a row of generic garment bags and a pile of shoes littering the floor. "I'd like to see the raspberry patch now."

Mr. Radcliff locked up the cupboard and escorted her outside, leaving the barn door unlocked. Moving around behind the barn, Mr. Radcliff led Maggie down a slippery path to the lower field. She spotted a large patch of raspberry bushes consisting of several rows with stout posts and wires holding up the dormant canes.

To reach the patch, she picked her way through knee-high grass peeking out of the snowdrifts.

"Careful," Mr. Radcliff said from a distance. "The last thing I need is to have a guest go and get herself all scratched up."

Again Maggie suspected that his chief concern was with financial liability. She felt a chill at his apparent indifference to the actual people involved in such situations.

Maggie inspected the branches closely for signs of fresh cutting. The wood had all scabbed over, proving that Kyle had lied to her. She sighed, wishing there was someone she could trust to help her find the poor young woman.

She climbed the hill to Mr. Radcliff. "If it's okay with you, I'd like to talk with your staff today to see if they know anything about Amanda."

"I suppose it can't hurt." He took out a pocket watch. "Be mindful that guests will soon be arriving. I hope you'll use discretion around them."

"I will."

"Now, if there's nothing else, I need to get back to my office to be sure we're ready to open on time."

"Nothing else right now," she said. "But thank you so much for your time."

He grunted noncommittally and hurried up the hill. At his office, they split up. As he closed his office door with a loud *thump,* she pondered his strange behavior. He had been helpful enough, but she felt that his interest in finding Amanda was rooted in the money he stood to lose if his establishment became a crime scene. And when money was involved, people could be driven to do desperate things.

Like cover up a kidnapping.

6

Just before noon, Maggie climbed the stairs to the manor house for the welcome lunch. She'd spent the last couple of hours visiting shops along Main Street. She'd had delightful conversations with the staff, and the shops were fascinating. She only wished she could have spent more time in them.

She stopped in the large foyer to take in the rustic beauty of the house. The home wasn't as grand or opulent as many 1800s city homes, but it had the country charm that was common for a farmhouse of the time. At her right sat a two-piece linen press cabinet. The manor house brochure described it as a stepback country cabinet, claiming that it was original to the house and that the exterior retained the original red grain flame paint in a rich oxblood hue. Maggie ached to open the doors to inspect the interior, but the cabinet sat behind a silk rope and a sign warned visitors not to touch any of the antiques.

To her left, a sitting room held an assortment of early American country furniture, the primitive style indicating that these items had been made before the mass production of home furnishings. These simple, unembellished pieces had probably been built by farmers to supplement their income during the dormant months, and Maggie was thankful to be surrounded by such stunning examples of bygone craftsmanship.

Maggie heard her friends' voices drifting from a room down the hall, and she headed in that direction, passing the sitting room, which held an early-nineteenth-century mahogany sofa with green cushions. It had a square back with down-swept wooden arm supports. Maggie was amazed by the pristine condition of the sofa and vowed to ask an employee if she could inspect it more closely later. Another silk rope was strung across the entrance to the sitting room, but she hoped that guests staying at Weatherly Manor would be granted access to more rooms than the tourists passing through.

She continued on to the dining room, where the women of the Somerset Harbor Historical Society sat around a long oak table with James at the head. Primitive oak benches provided seating on the sides and ladder-back armchairs sat at each end.

Everyone waved or called out to Maggie in greeting, and her heart gave a little flutter when she caught a glimpse of James's bright smile.

She turned to Mr. Radcliff, who stood off to the side. "Are you joining us for lunch?"

"No, Ms. Watson. I'm here to assign rooms and provide the group with an itinerary. I wish to do so *before* lunch is served." There was a trace of annoyance in his tone.

"Sounds perfect," Maggie said brightly as she took her seat.

"Let me first welcome you all to Weatherly Village." He smiled tightly, his expression still dour despite the gesture. "First I'll call out your names and give your room numbers. As the literature mailed to you mentioned, the rooms are all authentically accoutred, which means there are no locks on the doors. If for some reason you didn't leave your valuables at home, I have a safe in my office and will be glad to lock them up for you."

He lifted his clipboard.

"Okay, first on my list is Ruth Harper," he began, then made his way down the list until everyone had received a room assignment. "You'll find your clothing in your room waiting for you. We used the sizes you provided on your registration forms, but if you find the clothes don't fit properly, stop by my office on Main Street and I'll arrange for an exchange. The garments aren't original, but every effort has gone into making them as true to the period as possible. We do prefer that you wear your costume at least during the hours the village is open to the public. Please see our dressmaker if you get any tears or stains on your costume, and she will sort you out. We also ask that the ladies keep their hair and makeup simple and modest, for historical accuracy."

He faced Daisy, whose bright pink lipstick, sparkly eyeshadow, and liberally teased hairstyle could not have been further from the look he'd just described. "Mrs. Carter, since you'll be joining us in dressing up for the weekend but aren't staying in a room, we have kept room six vacant for you to change in."

Daisy clapped her hands. "I'm so excited. I can't wait to see my dress."

"I doubt it will be to your usual tastes. Women in the 1800s weren't known to wear neon colors as far as I know," James said with humor.

"Don't worry, my personality will liven it right up." She chuckled.

Maggie laughed with her friend, knowing that Daisy would find a way to stand out in a crowd even if she was given a plain white bedsheet to wear.

"You'll find a card with the clothing telling you which family member you are playing for the weekend," Mr. Radcliff broke in firmly over their amusement. "I realize assigning you a role to play is a surprise, but we didn't want anyone who felt they didn't have acting skills to stay away. You won't actually be performing for anyone, but with the details in the dossier, we feel you can better understand the clothing choices and your characters' roles within the household. When you are strolling the grounds, if you feel so inclined to interact with visitors while portraying your character, we encourage you to do so."

"How fun." Ina's eyes twinkled. At seventy-five, Ina Linton had a full head of cotton-white curls. She was petite and fit, and she didn't know the meaning of slowing down. "I wonder who I'll get to be."

Mr. Radcliff handed a stack of papers to Ruth to pass around the table. "This is your itinerary, which includes mealtimes and special group events personalized to the interests you expressed on the questionnaire you submitted when you made your reservations. As you can see, this afternoon at four o'clock, the schoolhouse will be open to you, and there will be supplies there for you to write out recipe cards and practice using a quill and ink. Men of Mr. Weatherly's stature would have had no need of recipe cards because cooking was largely considered women's work, but Mr. Bennett, if you would like to join the ladies, our staff will give you a formal letter template to use to practice your calligraphy skills as well. Penmanship was highly prized in both men and women of the time."

"I look forward to it," James said earnestly.

"Tomorrow is a recreational day. At ten in the morning, please gather in the side yard to join in our demonstration of the Game of Graces. Then after dinner, we will have a game night in the library and parlor that will be hosted by the guests assigned the roles of Mr. and Mrs. Weatherly for their staff and the town's tradespeople. Since several of you have expressed an interest in antiques on your questionnaires, you'll be happy to note that the game boards and pieces you'll play with are actual antiques."

"Ooh, games," June said. "I can't wait to see what they played in the 1800s."

"I can't wait either," Maggie said, feeling the stress of the last twenty-four hours melt away as she started to look forward to all the fun she and her friends would have over the weekend. Then she felt a stab of guilt as she remembered Amanda. How could she have fun with her friends when there was a young woman missing?

"You'll recognize some of the games, as many are still played today, but others will be a treat to learn," Mr. Radcliff said. "Now, one final thing. You should know that though the home has been wired with electricity, we will be cutting the power to the house so you can experience what life was like without it."

"Cutting the power seems a bit extreme, and maybe a bit of a hassle for you," James observed. "I think we could all just avoid using it if that would be easier."

"We've tried asking participants not to use the lights or outlets in the past, but there's always someone who doesn't comply and ruins the experience for others. And you'd be surprised how habituated we all are when it comes to turning on a light upon entering a room."

"That settles it," Daisy said. "I made the right choice bringing that motor home. I don't know what I'd do without my trusty hair dryer." She patted her big hairdo theatrically.

"Daisy, do you mind if we use the motor home's electricity to charge our phones and such? I'm all about the immersive experience, but it's important that our friends and family back home are able to reach us," Ruth said.

"Sure, but it'll cost ya." Daisy winked. "I'm only kidding. You're more than welcome to come down to the motor home to charge phones and use my hair dryer too."

Mr. Radcliff, apparently unamused by their banter, slipped another stack of papers from his clipboard and handed them to James. "This is the list of our rules and policies for the weekend. Please take one and pass the rest along, and familiarize yourself with the regulations we have in place for your safety and enjoyment. Please note you're free to roam the village throughout the day, but we ask you to remain in the manor house after dinner is served."

He clapped his hands, and Maggie jumped, spilling the papers onto the worn wooden tabletop.

"Are there any questions?" he asked.

A chorus of "noes" rose from the group gathered around the table.

"Then I'll let the cook know you're ready for lunch." He swept out of the room and disappeared down the hallway.

"Is he always so . . . formal?" James asked, pulling an exaggeratedly grumpy face in demonstration.

Maggie chuckled. "Yes. But he's been helpful too, so I'm grateful for that."

"I brought everyone up to speed on Amanda's situation," Daisy said.

"But we're unsure how embellished her telling of the situation was," James added. Daisy had a penchant for exaggeration.

Daisy leaned forward and jabbed his shoulder with her forefinger. "I'll have you know I stuck to the facts. Though the telling was colorful and included many sensory details, as all good stories should."

"Have you learned anything new this morning?" June asked.

Maggie mentioned the blood near the barn and Kyle's bloody clothes.

Daisy crossed her arms, her face dark. "I refuse to believe that anyone would want to hurt Amanda."

"That's the right attitude to have." June patted Daisy's arm. "I'm sure she'll turn up soon with no harm done."

"I agree," Ruth added in her usual no-nonsense tone as she pushed her glasses up on her nose. "We have to keep a positive attitude. And pray."

"Do you really think Kyle could be behind her disappearance?" Daisy asked Maggie.

"Yes, especially since the cobbler told Fran and me that he heard Kyle arguing with someone down by the barn on the night Amanda disappeared."

Daisy leaned in conspiratorially, resting her forearms on the smooth tabletop. "I heard this morning that a man here named Craig Baldwin is quite the flirt. He's the innkeeper at Weatherly Inn."

"I'll add his name to my list of suspects then. If Lily was right and Amanda was seeing someone new, maybe it was him." Maggie dug out her notebook and jotted down Craig's name under the name Daisy's niece had given her the previous night. "Lily suggested I look into Gabe Hendricks, the village blacksmith. Did either of you hear anything about him?"

The women shook their heads.

"If only I could be in multiple places at one time to keep track of Craig and Gabe—but my priority after lunch is to confront Kyle about his activities yesterday when Amanda went missing. I have reason to believe he was lying to me earlier."

"We can help," Ruth offered. "We'll keep our eyes on these young men."

"I don't want you to miss out on exploring the town."

"We can do both," Ruth said. "There are plenty of us. We can work in shifts and have time to explore the village too."

"It's good of you to help." Maggie looked around the table at the women who'd become such good friends to her.

"I'll get started on making a schedule right now." Ruth dug a pen from her purse and flipped over the itinerary.

"Leave it to Ruth to organize the group," June said. "What would we do without you as our society president?"

"Thank you, June. As long as you all want me to do the job, you'll never need to find out," Ruth replied with a twinkle in her eye.

"We'll always want you to do it, hon," Daisy said. "You're the best woman for it. I wouldn't want to try to keep us all in line. These ladies are a handful." They laughed.

A young woman wearing a black dress and white apron entered the room, her dark hair pulled into a low bun beneath a white frilly hat. She was carrying a wooden tray laden with a large platter of roast beef and bowls of carrots and mashed potatoes.

She set her burden on the sideboard and turned to the assembly with a small curtsy. "Pardon my interruption. We will be serving the meal family style. I'll place the dishes on the table and will return shortly with drinks. Our records indicate that no one has special dietary needs, so unless that is not the case, the meal shall begin."

When no one spoke up, she curtsied again and placed the bowls on the table. She retrieved the glistening beef roast and set the platter by James. "Sir, would you like to carve the meat?"

"It would be my pleasure," James said.

Maggie admired his polite and easy manner even while being given special treatment, something she knew the modest small-town alderman would normally refuse. She imagined what he would look like, sitting at the head of this table in his nineteenth-century attire. She hoped she would pull off the look in her own costume half as nicely as she was sure he would.

The maid curtsied and bustled from the room to retrieve their drinks.

"I've finished the schedule, and we can look at it after lunch." Ruth tucked the paper in her handbag. "Now let's enjoy this wonderful meal."

Ina spooned cooked carrots onto her plate and handed the bowl to Daisy. "How is Lily holding up?"

"She's keeping busy at the inn today," Daisy said. "I think that's got her spirits up a bit."

"I like that girl," Ina said. "I remember how spunky she was when she worked for you that summer."

Daisy lifted a spoonful of carrots from the bowl. "She has spirit and a good head on her shoulders. Jasmine raised her right."

"Then she'll come through this just fine." Ruth handed the mashed potatoes to Maggie.

She placed a huge dollop on her plate. "I hope the dressmaker was generous with the size of our clothes for the weekend. I know I didn't take into account all the calories we're going to consume eating as though we'll spend the day working the farm."

As if on cue, the maid returned with a glass pitcher of milk. "Though we don't keep cows on the estate, the Weatherly family did and would have had milk with their meals. We buy pasteurized milk for our guests, and it's chilled, but the family would have served it fresh from the cow, so it would have been warm." She handed the pitcher to Ruth, then disappeared again, with instructions for them to call into the kitchen if they needed anything else.

James met Maggie's gaze over the long table. "Have you seen much of the village?"

Maggie described the buildings she'd been able to visit that morning and the antiques she'd seen.

"I stopped at a few of the vendors' booths on the way in." He sliced the last of the juicy beef. "The most interesting one was a woman who was selling beeswax candles. Besides demonstrating how she made them, she had an observation beehive with her. It was fascinating to watch the bees at work."

"Bees—oh my goodness!" June said. "Won't they sting people?"

James passed the platter to Ina. "They're in an enclosed hive with thick acrylic glass for viewing so they can't escape."

"Thank goodness for that." Ina forked a slice of beef. "I want to visit the vendor who is churning and selling butter. There's nothing like the taste of fresh-churned butter. I used to make it all the time when I was a little girl."

"Why don't you make your own today?" Ruth asked.

"It's downright inconvenient, for one. The other thing is cost. It takes a lot of cream to make a single pound of butter. But *my*, is it good." She smacked her lips and passed the beef on to June.

June took a slice and set down the platter. "I read that this dining set is the same one used by the Weatherly family through the years. Each ding and scratch tells a story, and I'm so thrilled we get to be entertained with those stories all weekend. We're going to learn so much, and I think we'll gain a real appreciation for our ancestors."

James raised his glass of milk. "To a weekend of antiques and architecture."

"And butter!" crowed Ina.

They all laughed and clinked glasses, then dug into the succulent carrots, creamy potatoes, and fork-tender beef. When lunch ended, they went to their rooms to change.

Maggie walked around her small and modestly decorated room. A full-size bed—its frame painted bright red—took up most of the space. A flowery quilt in various shades of crimson covered the mattress, and matching curtains hung over the window. When this house was built, all of the quilts would have been skillfully hand-stitched by women of the era. Admiring the intricate handiwork reminded her of Fran's request to see pictures of their stay, and she snapped some quick photos of the room for her friend, being sure to get close-ups of the quilt and curtains.

A blue-gray brocade dress with a long cuirass bodice and contrasting trim lay on the bed. Because the material was so fine, she knew without reading her dossier that she would be playing one of the Weatherly women and not a servant.

She picked up the card and found she was to play Flora Weatherly, the lady of the house and mother of five boys and two girls. Maggie couldn't imagine having seven children, but she was excited to get into the spirit of the event. She quickly changed into the dress, which had a zipper hidden under the row of authentic-looking buttons that lined the back.

She looked in the large, gilded federal mirror, pleased to see the dress fit well and the blue-gray color worked well with her blonde hair. She wished she had longer hair to do the ensemble justice, but she settled for digging in her bag for a clip to hold back the top layer of her shoulder-length hair. She placed a white bonnet on her head and tied it below her chin, then transferred her phone and business cards to a velvet drawstring purse that had been provided to go with her costume. Finally, she squeezed her feet into the low-heeled leather shoes. As she stood, she grimaced at the tight fit and looked longingly at her tennis shoes.

She grabbed the long wool coat and sleek gloves. She wondered if they would keep her hands from freezing, but the sound of melting snow dripping from the eaves outside was an encouraging sign that the day was warming up. In the hallway, she had to swivel to keep from closing her skirt in the door—the first lesson, she supposed, in what would be a weekend-long education in wearing such attire.

Carefully descending the stairs, she found James standing in the foyer. He looked quite handsome in black trousers and a gray tweed jacket over a white shirt with black bow tie and a black-and-white houndstooth vest.

"Good afternoon, sir." She held out her gloved hand. "I'm Flora Weatherly."

"We can dispense with the formalities then, as you, dear Flora, are my wife."

The idea of being married to James sent a flush over her skin.

"No need to blush," he said. "I promise I'm quite the gentleman."

Maggie laughed but stopped abruptly when Daisy came down the stairs frowning. "What is it? What's wrong?"

"Look at me!" Daisy wailed as she ran her hands over a plain, washed-out gray gown with a modest ruffled collar and cuffs. "I'm Bertha Weatherly, William Weatherly's spinster sister and the local schoolmarm."

"You, a spinster schoolmarm?" James said, teasing in his voice. "Someone's got a good sense of humor."

Maggie didn't want to add to Daisy's distress, so she bit back her urge to laugh.

Daisy huffed and peered at Maggie. "And who are *you*?"

"Flora Weatherly," Maggie replied, a little timidly.

"You're so lucky," Daisy pouted.

"I don't know about lucky—Flora had seven kids! One sleepover with six of Emily's friends would be enough to tire me out for a week," Maggie said with a grin. Talking about her daughter's younger years made her happy, but her thoughts immediately turned to another young woman . . . Amanda. She'd been missing for nearly twenty-four hours now. Where could she be? Who was behind her disappearance?

And how much time did she have left?

7

With the warmth of the sun beating down on her wool coat, Maggie worked her way through the thick crowd with Daisy at her side. She appreciated the admiring glances from the visitors and the questions about the attire, but she also had to be mindful of the swish of her full skirt as she moved.

"My feet are killing me," Daisy groaned.

"I know. We haven't been in these costumes for more than an hour, and I already appreciate the challenges women in the 1800s faced with their uncomfortable clothing alone."

Daisy stopped at a pottery booth, where a man was shaping a vessel on a potter's wheel. He wore work overalls, a plaid shirt, and a tattered straw hat.

"Greetings, ladies," he said. "Care to try your hand at the wheel?"

Daisy made to take him up on the offer, then stopped short. "I can't. I'd love to try it, but I don't want to risk ruining these clothes."

"Besides," Maggie added, "what self-respecting schoolmarm would do such a thing in public?"

"Right." Daisy lifted her chin. "I might get dirty helping the children, but this is a man's work."

"My apologies, ladies. I meant no disrespect." The potter grinned and gave a little seated bow.

Maggie and Daisy continued down the street, passing a butter churner, a wood-carver, and a photographer who had wardrobe and backdrops to create vintage photo keepsakes.

"We need to get the group together to have our picture taken," Maggie suggested.

Daisy frowned.

"What's wrong?"

She plucked at her skirt. "I'm not sure I want a reminder of this plain-Jane outfit."

"But you would like a reminder of the visit, right?"

"I suppose that depends on what happens with Amanda."

"I'm sure she'll turn up soon. The police are handling it." Maggie hugged Daisy's shoulders. "Now let's cheer up for our visit to Lily."

"You're right. She doesn't need to see my worry."

They continued down the street until Maggie spied an oval sign with engraved letters stating *Weatherly Inn, established 1803.* It hung above the front door lintel of an unassuming two-story building painted yellow with rust-colored trim. A framed lunch menu was hanging outside the door alongside a schedule for daytime tours of the guest rooms. The inn was part of the daily tourist attractions only and wasn't available to overnight guests.

Maggie stepped up to the small portico covering the entry. She held the rustic wooden door for Daisy, and they slipped into the warmth of a large room with a floor-to-ceiling stone fireplace.

Jasmine sat in a painted wooden chair by the front window, watching Lily go about her scullery maid duties and idly working on a crochet project.

"My dress isn't so drab compared to Lily's. At least mine's got ruffles," Daisy said, plucking at her cuffs disconsolately.

Lily's dress was plain black cotton and was covered with a dingy gray apron. She'd pulled up her hair under a white cap, and she was busy feeding wood into the fireplace, one of the many jobs performed by a scullery maid.

Maggie remembered reading that scullery maids were the lowest-ranked servants, and in a small inn like this one, they would also take on the chambermaid's jobs. Lily would assist in the kitchen, scouring pots, cleaning vegetables and fish, and plucking poultry for visitors' lunches, but her nineteenth-century counterpart would have also carried water, lit fires, and even emptied and cleaned chamber pots in guest rooms. Fortunately, Lily would be spared that task since the inn didn't take guests.

"She looks happy, doesn't she?" Daisy asked.

"She does indeed." Maggie loved seeing Lily's animated face as she chatted with a couple who stood by the ash bucket she'd set on the stone hearth.

"Let's go talk to Jasmine."

Maggie followed Daisy across the room, taking in the white-washed wooden walls and large rag rugs, the glow from the fireplace leaving the room feeling warm and cozy.

Jasmine looked up from her crochet, and her face lit up at the sight of them. She wore jeans and a purple knit shirt and looked comfortable in her modern-day attire—far more comfortable than Maggie felt in her getup, and especially more so than Daisy, who kept tugging at her dress's neckline and shifting the bodice.

"Lily makes a fine scullery maid," Maggie said.

Jasmine beamed for a moment, but then worry overtook her expression. "Are you here to give us news about Amanda?"

"Not yet. I just wanted to see Lily."

Jasmine smiled fondly at her daughter. "I'm glad there have been so many visitors to keep her mind occupied until Amanda comes home."

"Have you heard anything more from her mother?" Maggie asked.

"I called her a few minutes ago and she's still not having any luck getting a flight home. She sounded so distraught, and I can't blame her. I told her to give me a call day or night if she needs any updates or someone to talk to."

"You're a good friend," Daisy said.

"I just wish I could do something for her, you know?" Jasmine stared out the window and suddenly sat up and peered closely at something out in the street. "That's odd. Kyle's mother is here. She's carrying a lunch box, so I guess Kyle must have forgotten it."

Maggie moved closer to the window. "Where do you see her?"

"The woman in the red coat. Her name is Hannah Jensen."

"I need to talk to her about Kyle," Maggie said, already working her way through a fresh crowd of tourists to the door.

She slipped outside and wound her way through the visitors in the street to catch up with Hannah.

"Mrs. Jensen?" Maggie called out.

The woman turned and brushed a lock of her chin-length salt-and-pepper hair behind her ear as Maggie hurried forward. Even with a bulky coat, Maggie could tell the woman was rail-thin, quite the opposite of burly Kyle.

"Can I help you?" she asked, looking wary.

"I hope so." Maggie introduced herself, taking care to mention her connection to Jasmine. "Have you heard that Amanda Caldwell has gone missing?"

"Amanda? No." Hannah shook her head hard, and the strand of hair she'd so carefully tucked behind her ear fell free. "What happened?"

Maggie quickly explained what she knew. "I'm trying to help find her."

Hannah frowned. "It's horrible that she's missing. She's such a sweet girl, and she was so good for my son."

"I hear they were together for quite some time."

"Yes, and the breakup has taken a toll on him."

"I totally understand," Maggie said. "I have a teenage daughter, and I've helped her through relationship issues in the past. Young love can be complicated."

Hannah took a breath and slowly exhaled. "Their breakup was so devastating to Kyle. And to me, honestly. He's always had a temper like his dad, but when Kyle was with her he kept it under control. Since they've broken up, he's been in a royally bad mood. Out all hours of the night and generally a real crank when he's home."

Maggie offered a reassuring smile. "Like I said, I have a daughter, so I don't know much about raising boys, but I didn't think they ever spent much time at home."

"He doesn't, but at least before the breakup he didn't stay out so late, and when he was gone I took comfort in knowing he was with someone who could keep him out of trouble." She sighed.

Maggie felt sorry for Kyle's mother. He was clearly breaking her heart. Maggie wished she didn't have to tell this concerned woman about her suspicions, but it couldn't be avoided.

"You should know he threatened Amanda the other day," Maggie said. "He said if he couldn't have her, no one could."

"Don't tell me you think Kyle had something to do with Amanda's disappearance." She put up her hands as if to ward off Maggie's suspicions. "No. Not my son. He might have a temper, and he's trying to find his way in the world right now, but he'd never hurt someone. Especially not Amanda."

For Hannah's sake, Maggie wished she shared the woman's confidence in Kyle. "He was also seen arguing with someone in the very spot where Amanda's mittens were found, but he told me he'd gone home where he stayed with you all night."

"What time did he tell you he went home?" Hannah chewed on her lower lip.

"He claimed he went home straight from work. I assume you live in town, which would put his arrival time around five thirty, maybe six."

"Oh dear." Hannah clutched her chest.

"What is it, Hannah?" Maggie could barely breathe when she saw the stricken look on Hannah's face.

"I stayed up late last night because I was worried about him. It must have been at least midnight before I went to bed, and he wasn't home yet."

The two mothers stared at each other.

What else had Kyle lied about?

8

A couple of hours later, Maggie hurried into the one-room schoolhouse. She found all of her friends seated at wooden desks with scrollwork cast-iron bases. All but Daisy, who stood in front of the room with a middle-aged woman wearing round spectacles.

"Our blackboard—" The woman broke off midsentence and turned at the sound of Maggie entering. She gave Maggie a disapproving glare.

The others turned to look at Maggie.

"Sorry I'm tardy," she said, slipping into the closest desk and shedding her coat.

The woman pivoted to the blackboard mounted on rough walls next to a large potbelly stove and wrote *Mrs. Eliza Kaufman* in large cursive letters, then turned back to face them again. "As I was saying, our blackboard is an authentic slate board from the early 1800s. By the middle of the nineteenth century, almost every classroom in America had a blackboard like this one. And you'll find it interesting to note that the slate for these boards came from quarries right here in our fair state, and was shipped all across the country to be used in schoolrooms nationwide."

She handed her chalk to Daisy. "Now, your teacher, Miss Bertha Weatherly, will write the recipe on the board. You may use the calligraphy books I have distributed to practice different styles of writing using a quill and ink."

Daisy made a face at her friends at being called "Miss Bertha" but stifled it when Mrs. Kaufman cast a stern look in her direction.

"You'll find two pieces of paper," she continued, "along with a quill and an inkwell on your desk. Use the plain paper to blot the end of your quill so you can write neatly, and the lined paper to try your hand at writing in this fashion. The recipe is for a gingerbread cake, which you will see being made in the manor house kitchen after this class. You may take the recipe home with you as a keepsake."

She looked over her spectacles at Daisy. "Go ahead, Miss Weatherly."

"Oh, right, that's me." Daisy tried to look studious, but she didn't quite manage to keep a straight face as she picked up a note card and faced the board.

"If we were being completely historically correct, we would be using slates for your writing, as paper was too expensive to use in a classroom back in the day," Mrs. Kaufman said, surveying them with a sour look on her face. "However, these days the table has turned, and paper is less expensive than slates. If you have any questions, now is the time to ask."

She looked them over, and Maggie was sure that if anyone else had a question, they were as afraid to ask as she was.

Mrs. Kaufman gave a firm nod, and her glasses slid to the end of her nose. "You may begin."

Maggie turned her attention to the quill and paper before her and soon discovered how much she had taken modern ballpoint pens for granted. She tried her best not to splotch the paper but dropped a few dots of ink. The room was silent for a while, but once the no-nonsense tone of Mrs. Kaufman's lecture had faded away, a hum of chatter arose. Daisy made a show of playing schoolmarm, looking down her nose at everyone's work and playfully scolding James when she caught him sticking out his tongue in concentration as he fumbled with the quill. When they'd all finished, Mrs. Kaufman returned to the front of the room, looking displeased as she waited for all the chatter to die down.

She held up a certificate. "Today's writing award goes to Mrs. North, our town's milliner." She thrust out a hand to Ina like a game show host displaying a prize.

Ina looked around, confused, before she remembered her character name and clapped her hands with glee.

"Please come up for your certificate, Mrs. North."

Ina strode to the front, her deep green velvet skirt swishing over the wide floorboards.

Mrs. Kaufman shook Ina's hand. "I suspect your writing skills are due to all of your intricate sewing work."

"My what?" Ina said.

"The sewing work you do when designing hats, madam. As milliner, surely your meticulous handiwork is essential to creating a quality product."

"Oh, that. Sure, I'm a fine melon baller. Whatever you say!" She winked at her friends behind the schoolmarm's back.

Mrs. Kaufman raised a hand to her chest in shock. "Yes . . . well, here you are." She handed Ina the certificate.

Leave it to Ina to fluster the unflappable schoolmarm.

Mrs. Kaufman clapped her hands smartly. "Now, if you'll all hurry over to the manor kitchen, our cook will instruct you in the fine art of using a woodstove."

They all got up, donned their outerwear, and strolled out of the building.

"Congratulations, Ina," Maggie said. "Or should I say *Mrs. North.*"

"I suppose I should get used to being called Mrs. North. They seem to take their acting seriously here." Ina chuckled.

Maggie turned to Ruth and June. "And who are you two playing?"

"I'm Dorothy Fairfax," Ruth said. "You may be able to tell

by my simple, modest dress that I'm the preacher's wife."

"And I'm Rachael Samuels." June ran a hand down her cotton print dress. "The farmer's wife."

"Don't dawdle or you'll delay dinner," Mrs. Kaufman's shrill voice called after them. "The cook is waiting on you to do the demonstration."

The group members exchanged glances, then hurried down Main Street to the manor house. They agreed to meet in the kitchen for the cooking demonstration, then split up to deposit their winter things in their rooms.

The moment Maggie pushed open the kitchen door, warmth and the smell of fresh biscuits wafted out and made her stomach rumble in spite of her huge lunch.

The cook looked up from a cast-iron stove and wiped her hands on the red gingham apron she wore over a drab brown-and-gold-patterned dress. The skirt was full and fell to the floor, and the cinched waist accentuated the woman's plump middle. A white lacy handkerchief poked out of her sleeve at the wrist and brightened up the working-class dress.

She brushed strands of graying hair from her face with the back of her hand. "Good afternoon. I'm Ingrid Baldwin. As you may have guessed, I'm the cook."

Maggie introduced herself, and since she was the first person to arrive, she decided to ask the cook if she knew anything about Amanda.

"I did see her around the kitchen, since she was a maid here." Ingrid crossed to a large island and pulled a bowl of dough closer. "She peeled a few vegetables yesterday and cleaned up for me, but work?" Ingrid stopped talking and bit her lip for a moment. "I don't want to speak badly of the girl, but she didn't really want to do much except stand around with a dreamy look on her face and talk about getting married."

Maggie struggled to keep her surprise from showing. "Is she engaged?"

"I'm not one for chatting at work, so I didn't ask, and she didn't say. But I got the impression that she was in love with someone and would be getting married soon. She kept yakking on about filling her house with antiques like the ones we have here." Ingrid snorted. "No way could she afford antiques like these unless she was marrying a rich guy. When I said as much, she clammed up, and I got the feeling she was keeping a big secret."

She punched down the fluffy dough, and Maggie watched it collapse like a balloon losing air.

"Maybe you should talk to Oliver Dorn about Amanda," Ingrid said, as if the idea had just occurred to her. "He's the village caretaker. He's lived on the property for ten years or so, and he knows everyone and everything that goes on in the village."

"Thank you for the suggestion. Where would I find him?"

Ingrid glanced at an English fusee clock with a porcelain-covered dial and solid redwood case hanging on the kitchen's brick wall.

"At this time of day," she said, returning her attention to her dough, "he'll be hiding out in his cottage. He's not fond of people, especially visitors. When the village is open, he only comes out at night to do his job."

Maggie found it interesting that he worked at night. If Amanda had been in the village last night, he might have seen her.

Ingrid planted her hands on the rim of the thick stoneware bowl. Maggie was tempted to request a closer inspection of the bowl to see the maker's mark, but her friends filed into the kitchen at that moment.

Ingrid introduced herself, then continued, "First, forget the hierarchies of your character roles, since the gentleman and lady of the house wouldn't be involved in labor, but we don't want you to miss out on the experience." She looked at James. "Sir, I need you to go out back and chop wood for the stove."

James started for the door. As he stepped outside, a young maid dressed in attire similar to Lily's bustled past him into the room and approached Ingrid.

Ingrid frowned. "About time, girl."

The rotund girl, whose name tag read Tammy Prichard, looked like she wanted to retort, but she forced a smile onto her face instead. Maggie guessed that the abrupt change in attitude came from the customer-service classes Mr. Radcliff had mentioned.

Ingrid addressed the entire group. "We'll need eggs for the gingerbread cake, and I need two volunteers to accompany Tammy to the chicken coop."

"As the farmer's wife, maybe I should do it," June volunteered.

"Yes, good. And take our dear preacher's wife with you, as she has a chicken coop of her own and should know how to collect the eggs too."

Daisy eyed the woodstove. "I don't know how you cook on this thing. I have my share of challenges using a modern gas oven."

Ingrid grabbed a pan of water and joined Daisy. "Ovens in a woodstove don't often heat evenly, creating hot spots that make your pot or pan placement critical. If you'll open the door, I'll show you where to place this pan of water near the firebox, so it absorbs some of the excess heat and helps eliminate those hot spots."

Daisy grabbed pot holders and pulled open the door.

"It's also important to use oak for the fire. It burns clean and slow, so you don't have to use as much of it or worry about it contaminating the food." Ingrid placed the pan. "You also have to learn how to use the dampers and regulators to control the heat."

"And you can teach us how to do that in an hour or less?" Daisy asked. "*And* make a recipe?"

"I sure can. But I can't account for how long it will take you to learn, so roll up your sleeves, ladies. You're about to discover there's far more to life in the 1800s than wearing a pretty dress."

9

With a gingerbread cake baked and the lovely smell of cinnamon and cloves perfuming the air, the friends went to their own rooms to freshen up for dinner. After Maggie had washed up, she found that she was too antsy to sit around and wait for the meal. She grabbed her coat and headed out into the chilly night to make a quick visit to Oliver Dorn as Ingrid had suggested.

His cottage was a typical Cape Cod with gray clapboard siding and red trim. She mounted the small wooden stoop out front and knocked on the painted red door.

A balding man with a bushy white beard answered the door. He reminded Maggie of Santa Claus, but he was dressed in worn modern-day overalls over a denim shirt that had faded from many washings.

"Help you?" The suspicion in his eyes made him look far less like Santa Claus.

"Mr. Dorn, I'm Maggie Watson. I've been asked to look into the disappearance of Amanda Caldwell."

"Bad business, that," he said, his face clouded. "But I don't know why you want to talk to me about it. I didn't hear or see a thing."

"You live very near the barn where she went missing around four yesterday. . ." Maggie let the implication hang in the air.

"When the village is open I often nap during the day, as my work frequently gets done after everyone has gone home for the night."

"But not today?"

"Nope. What with the manor house being open for guests, we have extra staff on duty who will take on many of my cleaning duties tonight. Means I'll get to bed at a reasonable time and don't need a nap."

"How nice for you," she said and meant it. The man looked to be in his seventies, and she hated to think he had to work late hours on a regular basis. "Would you mind if I asked you a few questions about the village and the workers here?"

He seemed to think it over, then moved aside so she could enter. She quickly glanced around the main room, which contained a small kitchen, dining space, and sitting area by a tall stone fireplace.

He closed the door firmly, drawing her attention. "I made a fresh pot of coffee. Would you like some?"

"Thank you. That would be perfect to take off the chill."

He crossed the room to the kitchen consisting of a single wall of cabinets and an ancient stove and refrigerator that she suspected had been in the cottage since the 1950s. She turned to examine the rest of the room. Snowshoes and cross-country skis sat in a large wooden crate by the door. The ceilings were low, with thick wood beams painted a bright white to match the walls. The stone fireplace took up the far wall and had a rough-hewn mantel mounted in the middle of the stone. An antique rifle hung above it, oil lamps sat at each end, and a clock took center stage.

The clock drew her interest. From where she stood, it looked like a Louis XVI mantel clock. It looked out of place in this humble cottage, and she assumed it was a reproduction. She crossed the room to take a closer look, passing the worn sofa and leather easy chair. Up close, she saw it was constructed of black marble and doré brass castings. The materials and components seemed to be of the highest quality, which she did not associate with most reproductions.

She spun to face the kitchen.

"This is an actual Louis XVI clock," she said with breathless delight.

Oliver turned to look at her. "Ayup. Passed down through my family."

"There's a Federal eagle on the pendulum, so it's one of the rare Parisian clocks made for the American market. They often added motifs of the new country to appeal to New Englanders."

"Made in 1786." He crossed the room with their coffee.

She took the proffered mug. "Do you have any idea of the value of this clock?"

"You mean besides the value I place on my family's past?"

"Yes, besides that," she replied, feeling chastised for having thought of only the monetary value of such an item.

"I had it appraised once. They told me it was worth a couple grand."

"Then that must have been quite some time ago. I'm no expert, but I own an antiques shop in Somerset Harbor, and I'd say this lovely piece would bring at least $5,000."

He arched a bushy eyebrow. "Nice to know. If I decide to sell, I'll let you know. Though I don't see that happening."

She fished a business card from her small purse and handed it to him. "My number's on there."

He gestured at a round oak dining table with white painted chairs. "Go ahead and sit."

She placed her cup on the table and pulled out a chair, noting with an antique lover's eye the chipped whitewash exposing an undercoat of red paint that had been the original color a hundred or more years ago. "How long have you lived here?"

"Eleven years this June." He scowled as though the figure troubled him.

"Being a caretaker for such old buildings must be a challenge."

"It is, but I've been a handyman all my life, and it's what I like to do. Way back when, I even volunteered to help keep this place in shape free of charge. Then when they had enough money to hire a caretaker, they came to me, and it seemed like a natural fit."

"And was it?" She picked up her mug. "Do you like the job?"

"I don't much like the crowds, but keeping history alive, that I like." He took a long sip of his coffee. "But you didn't come here to talk about me."

"You're right," she said. "Can you think of any reason Amanda might have gone missing?"

His frown deepened, but he didn't speak.

"Seems like you have an idea, but you're hesitant to share."

He blew on the rim of his cup, sending steam curling up around his face. "Don't want to get no one in trouble."

"Trouble or not, if you can help find Amanda, wouldn't it be worth it?"

He leaned forward. "I heard that money was taken yesterday from the cashbox at the apothecary."

"Money? You're sure?" she asked, surprised that Mr. Radcliff hadn't mentioned the missing money when he'd had ample opportunity to do so.

"Yeah. Positive. When Donald went to close out the cashboxes for the night, the apothecary's box was short. Wasn't a huge sum of money 'cause they'd only filled the boxes so they could make change this weekend, but still it was short."

"Interesting, but how is it related to Amanda?"

"I thought maybe she saw who took the money and was going to report him." His eyes narrowed. "Her former boyfriend—that Kyle kid who's working down at the barn—talks an awful lot about what he'd do if he had some cash. He said he'd buy her a big ring, and then he knew she'd agree to marry him. He

didn't much like other guys looking at her, either. Warned a few of them off."

"Warned as in threatened?"

Oliver rubbed the whiskers on his chin. "Yeah, you could say threatened."

"Do you remember who the guys were?"

"Nah, was just a group of them I saw him lay into when I went to get lunch the other day."

Another strike against Kyle. But had Kyle stolen the money, and had Amanda seen him do it? Or had it been someone else?

The one thing Maggie kept hearing from people was how much Kyle loved Amanda, and that didn't jive with her suspicions. Still, even his mother had confirmed that he had a temper, so maybe when other young men had shown interest in Amanda, Kyle's temper had gotten the better of him and he'd made some rash decisions. No matter what, she needed to follow up on the missing money since it could be a link to Amanda's whereabouts. "Have you heard any rumors about who could have stolen the money?"

"I haven't heard anything else, but if you want to know more about it, you should talk to Donald."

"Mr. Radcliff, you mean. What do you think of him as a manager? Do you think he likes his job?"

"Sure, why?"

"He's been a little cranky."

"Typical Donald. He's an okay guy, but his good mood flies the coop the minute anything goes wrong. I saw that yellow tape out by the barn today. I bet he's having a real hissy fit over that." Oliver chuckled.

Maggie smiled at Oliver. He might be a bit of a recluse, but he was a likable person all the same. And maybe she'd think the same thing of Mr. Radcliff if he wasn't having a "hissy fit," as Oliver called it.

Maggie took a long drink of her coffee and savored the wonderful nutty taste. She'd seen an old-fashioned percolator on the stovetop and suspected that it was the reason for the intense flavor.

"Have you heard anything about Amanda dating a guy who works here?" she asked.

"No, but then she only started this week, so maybe it hasn't gotten around yet."

"If she was, can you think of anyone she might date? Maybe someone she'd want to keep secret."

He turned his cup in circles on the table leaving wet rings. "The innkeeper, Craig Baldwin. He's been here going on five years now, and I've seen him take a shine to every young maid we hire who's passable in the looks department." Oliver took a sip of his coffee. "Yeah, I think he'd be your top candidate."

Maggie didn't mention that Craig was already on her list, but she struck up a casual conversation about the village until she finished her coffee and got up to leave.

At the door, she slipped on her coat. "I'm staying at the manor house this weekend, so if you think of anything else, you should be able to find me there."

"Enjoy your experience. Most people do."

"You sound a little incredulous."

He shrugged. "The place is drafty and cold. The clothes are cumbersome, as I'm sure you've already figured out. Especially the big dresses like the one you're wearing. Give me a cozy cottage, my work clothes, and a cup of hot coffee, and I'm a happy man."

"With the exception of your mantel clock, you like the simple things in life."

"Exactly."

"Well, thanks for your time." She exited the building into

frosty twilight, and after sitting in the warm cottage with a cup of hot coffee, the air felt especially cold as she hurried toward the manor house.

On the way, she noticed the lights were still on at the inn even though the village was mostly empty of tourists since it was nearly closing time. With Oliver having just mentioned Craig Baldwin, Maggie decided that now would be a good time to speak with him privately.

She found the man she assumed was Craig standing behind a scarred wooden reception desk right inside the inn's front door. He was tall, maybe six five, had broad shoulders under his white shirt and striped waistcoat, and wore his thick jet-black hair slicked back.

"I'm sorry, but we're closed for the day," he said, a practiced smile on his face.

She checked his name tag to confirm his identity before introducing herself.

"What can I help you with, Ms. Watson? Or should I say, Mrs. Weatherly." He leaned against the scarred wood countertop.

"I guess you recognize my costume."

"I've seen that dress on a bunch of women, and might I say, you wear it especially well." He flashed a winsome grin at her.

With his good looks and blatant compliments, she believed Oliver's assertion that he was a flirt, but there was a desperate air to his charm that told her he wasn't often successful at eliciting dates. "I wondered if we could talk about Amanda Caldwell."

His face fell, and she knew she'd struck a nerve.

She forged ahead. "Several people today have told me that you might have been dating her. Is that true?"

"That's ridiculous!" He pushed off the counter.

"I've heard that you show interest in the younger girls who work here."

"Not that it's any of your business, but I'm only twenty-five. That isn't too old to go out with an eighteen-year-old like Amanda."

"You must have talked to her, then, if you know her age. Maybe since she's friends with Lily, she stopped in here and you got to talking. One thing led to another."

"I don't know who you are, lady, but what I do or don't do is none of your business." He eyed her, his gaze now sharp and angry.

"I'm sorry," she said soothingly. "I might have come across a little too intense. I'm just concerned about Amanda."

"As is everyone else around here." He sounded sincere, but she had to remember that the people who worked at Weatherly Village spent all day playing a part. She had to question whether Craig's concern was genuine or just an act.

He lifted a hinged section of the counter and strode to the door. "If you'll excuse me, the village is closing for the night, and I need to lock up. Which means it's time for you to get over to the manor house before they lock you out for the night."

Maggie didn't want to leave, but she could tell he wouldn't reveal anything else. However, that didn't mean she couldn't hang around outside for a few minutes to see what he did when he left the inn.

Pretending to return to the house, she crossed the street and glanced over her shoulder. He'd moved away from the door and window, so she ducked into the space between the dressmaker's shop and the printshop. The streetlights didn't reach that area, and she hid in the shadows, feeling like a criminal. She didn't have to remain there very long, however. Craig came outside, locked the door, looked both ways, and then rushed across the street, passing right in front of her.

She held her breath and counted to twenty before following. He stomped toward the manor house, his boots punching through the thick blanket of snow. Instead of going to the front door, he circled around the side.

What on earth is he up to?

Following a man into the dark wasn't something she did often. She took a deep breath and blew it out to calm her anxious feelings. She hurried down the sidewalk and onto the path he'd taken through the side yard.

She rounded the corner in time to see him enter the kitchen door at the back of the house. Maggie silently picked her way through the shrubbery abutting the house to peek through a window, her dress getting tangled in branches and slowing her down. She found Craig talking to Ingrid, his body language tense and agitated. He suddenly grabbed Ingrid by the arm and marched her across the room. He pressed on the brick wall behind the stove.

A secret door popped open, and the pair disappeared inside.

10

Maggie's mind raced. Had Craig taken Amanda and now Ingrid too?

Not on my watch. She turned the doorknob slowly to keep from making noise. Pressing open the squeaky kitchen door, she waited for Craig to come barreling back out of the secret door. She inhaled deeply of the scent she thought was roasting chicken with rosemary. When she thought it safe, she eased inside and closed the door, then slipped across the room. She approached the brick wall and ran her fingers over the rough masonry in the same spot where Craig had gotten the door to swing open.

Time ticked by as she moved her fingers in a pattern across the brick. Suddenly, one of them gave way, and she pushed hard. The brick sank into the wall, and the door popped open, revealing a set of stairs. She entered and closed the door behind her, waiting with bated breath for sounds of movement from above.

One minute passed. Two. Three. She thought she could make out the sounds of muffled voices, but they were faint and far away.

Rough wooden stairs led steeply upward in a spiral. Light glowed dimly from a punched tin sconce halfway up the curved stairwell, but the stairs beyond were shrouded in darkness. Growing impatient, she twitched up her skirt, then carefully placed her foot on the first stair, making sure she had a solid footing before starting up. She repeated this on each step until she moved past the lantern and it grew too dark to see her feet.

The voices from above grew louder as she approached, the unmistakable sounds of a barely contained argument stilling her feet. She strained to see ahead, but the spiral staircase continued upward in total darkness. She urged herself forward, even if it meant doing so blindly. She pressed her hands against the walls and started up. After another twist of the stairwell, she clearly heard Craig's and Ingrid's raised voices.

"You may be the Weatherly heir, Craig Baldwin—"

"*Illegitimate* heir," he interrupted Ingrid.

What? He's an heir? Maggie leaned in closer, her breath catching in her chest.

"Well, that goes without saying. If you were a legitimate heir, we'd be living in this house instead of serving here while trying to find a way to lay claim to your inheritance."

"Whatever," he said.

"I don't like your attitude, young man," Ingrid snapped. "I'm running the show here and don't you forget it. Stepson or not, I won't hesitate to kick you out of my house and cut you out of the plan."

"Geez, Ingrid. Give it a rest. I get it. Honestly. I'm just worried that the missing money and the whole Amanda thing will ruin things for us."

"What happens to Amanda should be none of your concern."

"But what about that nosy lady poking around?" he asked. "She thinks I had something to do with Amanda. I don't like her butting into my business."

Me. He means me.

"Don't you worry about that. I'll take care of her. C'mon now. I have dinner to get on the table. If everything goes according to plan, we'll have enough money soon, and I'll be able to leave this miserable job."

Maggie hurried back down the steps as fast as her bulky dress allowed.

Please, please don't let me fall.

Nearing the bottom, she stumbled, but she righted herself by grabbing onto the wall.

She wasn't going to wait around to find out whether she'd made enough noise to attract attention. She pushed through the opening and into the kitchen, where she quietly settled the door into place. She flew across the kitchen and into the hallway leading to the front of the house.

She heard her friends' voices coming from the sitting room, and she paused to lean against the wall and catch her breath. Perspiring from running, she took off her coat and breathed deeply.

Her mind went to the tidbit she'd overheard about Craig being an heir to the Weatherly estate, and Ingrid's chilling promise: *I'll take care of her.* Ingrid had seemed kind—if a little brusque—in the kitchen, but the woman Maggie had just overheard was short-tempered and cruel. Maggie didn't have a clue what Ingrid meant about "taking care of" her, but she knew the pair were up to something, and by the sound of it, it was something sinister. Maggie had to find out if it had anything to do with Amanda's disappearance. Since it sounded like Ingrid was in charge, it would be a good idea to follow her tonight. Maggie would have to eat her meal quickly, dress warmly in her normal clothes, and hide outside to watch the kitchen. It would be a cold night for it, but she felt compelled to follow any lead she had in order to help bring Amanda home.

A loud burst of laughter cut through the air. It warmed Maggie's heart to know that her friends were having a good time on their trip. She vowed not to share the latest news or bring up Amanda's disappearance during dinner unless one of them asked. She wanted them to continue to enjoy their time together. She took a final breath and slowly let it out before entering the sitting room.

"There you are!" James exclaimed. "Where have you been?"

"Following up on a lead," she said vaguely.

His eyebrow went up. "A lead you're not going to share with us?"

"Not just yet." She took a seat between Ina and June on the mahogany sofa. With their full skirts, not a bit of cushion was visible.

"So what's everyone been up to today?" she asked, dodging any further questions.

"I'd rather find out what you've been doing," June whispered. "But I'll be patient."

Maggie smiled at June. She appreciated her friends' support.

"I had the most marvelous day," Ina announced. "I shopped the vendors and bought a beeswax candle, plus the hand-churned butter I was craving, which Mr. Radcliff is storing in the refrigerator for me."

"I think I'll have to get some for myself before we leave," Maggie said, imagining the fresh butter melting on a piece of toast. "What about the antiques? Did everyone enjoy seeing them as much as I did?" Maggie thought about the stepback cupboard. "I've always had an interest in primitive furniture, but with pieces like that cupboard in the foyer, I've officially fallen completely head over heels for this style."

The gathered friends launched into conversation about antiques they had seen throughout the day and carried the pleasant talk all the way through dinner. By the time they'd finished the gingerbread cake they'd baked that afternoon, Maggie's mood had lifted, and she was ready to stand in the cold and investigate her lead on Amanda with a renewed fervor.

She pushed away from the table. "I need to go down to the motor home to update Daisy, Lily, and Jasmine on what I know about Amanda." Maggie felt bad about not sharing all of her plans for the evening, but she wasn't being entirely untruthful.

She would have to stop by the motor home to get the keys to Jasmine's car so she could follow Ingrid. Maggie lifted her foot. "But before I go anywhere, I'm headed upstairs to change. I'm not going to try to navigate the cold slush in these shoes."

She set off a wave of talk about the footwear, and as her friends chatted, she slipped into the hallway. In her room, she hung the gown in an armoire and put on her street clothes, which included heavy boots and a down jacket. She grabbed her hat and mittens and hurried down the stairs.

Coat in hand, James waited by the front door. "I'm going with you."

She appreciated his chivalry, but she couldn't allow him to accompany her. "I need to do this alone."

"I don't like the thought of you wandering around at night on your own."

"I won't be wandering," she replied and hoped it was true.

"But you're not just going to the motor home, are you?"

She realized with a flush how often she underestimated his ability to see her real motives. "You got me," she replied sheepishly.

"Then I'm coming with you, and it would be helpful if you brought me up to speed on where we're going."

"Not in here where we can be overheard."

He slipped on his jacket and opened the door for her. "After you."

She headed into the night, her breath coming in little puffs in the frigid air. When he closed the door, she faced him and told him about Ingrid and Craig. "I plan to follow Ingrid tonight to see if she leads me to Amanda. Because there's a greater chance of two people being seen, I'd like to go alone."

"I understand," he said, but his tone said he didn't like it.

"What? You aren't going to try to talk me out of it or tell me to call the police?"

He frowned into her face, then sighed. "It's a strong lead, and I think you need to follow it. But if it gets dangerous, I want you to promise to call the sheriff's office right away. If you don't promise, I'll insist on joining you."

"I promise." She tightened the scarf around her neck.

"Good," he said. "Do you even know what time Ingrid is supposed to leave?"

"I couldn't ask without raising suspicion."

"Then you could be standing in the cold for hours," he protested.

She held up her mittens. "I'm dressed warmly. I'll be fine."

"If she doesn't leave the building soon, please don't risk your health by staying out here."

"I won't," she assured him, but she knew she would have to be close to frostbite before she would return to the house without any new information. She turned to leave.

"Do me a favor," James called out.

She looked over her shoulder.

"Text me every so often to let me know you're okay." His lips tipped up in a smile that warmed her heart and chased away the cold.

"If I can get a signal. It's sketchy around here." She reconsidered asking him to join her, but instead she reminded herself that two of them were more likely to be spotted, and she couldn't afford the risk. Neither could Amanda.

She hurried down the steps. Snow that had melted earlier was turning to ice. She thought of the same thing happening on the roads and said a silent prayer for the safety of anyone traveling them tonight—herself included. She made a quick trip to the motor home. After providing vague answers to Daisy's questions, she managed to secure Jasmine's keys in her pocket and return to the manor house. Not knowing which door Ingrid would depart through, Maggie searched for a hiding place where she could see the front entrance and anyone who exited the back and came through the side yard.

Tall evergreen shrubs on the far side of the small yard would do nicely for a stakeout spot. She slogged through the crust of frozen snow and darted behind the shrubs. The only sound she heard in the secluded village was an owl hooting in a nearby tree. Time ticked by slowly and cold seeped into her body. She stomped her boots on the snow and patted her hands together to keep warm. Fifteen minutes that felt like an hour passed without a sign of Ingrid. Maggie tried to text James to tell him she was still watching the house and nothing was amiss, but she didn't have a signal. Another quarter hour passed, and she moved around the area to try James again, but her phone had zero bars, and she hoped he didn't come looking for her.

Finally, five minutes later, she heard footsteps crunching on the snow in the backyard. She held her breath as she waited for the person to appear.

Wearing a bulky green parka, Ingrid swung around the corner and trudged toward the gate. She had a large tote slung over her shoulder, and Maggie couldn't help but wonder about the contents. She thought of the conversation she had overheard. Ingrid seemed intent upon some plan to get more money. Was Ingrid the one who'd stolen from the apothecary, and would she be willing to take even more drastic action to serve her selfish aims?

When Ingrid reached Main Street, Maggie set off in pursuit. At the road, Maggie stopped behind a large pine tree and peeked around the massive trunk. Ingrid had walked to the far end of the shops. She suddenly stopped and looked around, as if she sensed Maggie's presence.

Maggie ducked behind the tree and held her breath so the

warm vapor from her mouth wouldn't give her away. When she grew desperate for air, she glanced again and was relieved to see Ingrid had continued down the street.

Maggie whooshed out her breath and then gulped in air before scurrying down the road. She took her time and kept out of the pools of lamplight in case Ingrid turned, but Ingrid marched straight to the gate and through the turnstile without pausing a second time.

Maggie arrived at the gate in time to see Ingrid slide into the old blue sedan Maggie had seen first thing in the morning. The moment Ingrid backed out and drove toward the exit, Maggie ran toward Jasmine's minivan. She lost her footing several times and had to slow down, but soon she was in the van and driving out of the lot with the headlights off.

At the road, Maggie had to turn on the lights, but she trailed far enough behind to keep Ingrid from becoming suspicious. She cranked up the heat to thaw out her chilled body and trailed the sedan into the nearby town of Weatherly. Maggie slowed to hang back even farther, taking corners only once she was sure Ingrid had plenty of time to clear the area.

After several turns, Ingrid pulled into the driveway of a small bungalow. Maggie killed her headlights and stopped to watch Ingrid climb from the car and unlock the front door.

Maggie eased the minivan slowly down the road. When she felt she'd driven as close as she could without Ingrid seeing her, Maggie parked and turned off the engine. She opened the window to keep from fogging the windshield. Cold wind whistled into the interior, and Maggie shivered. She took a moment to text James her location and to tell him that she was fine.

He responded. *So glad to hear from you. Mr. Radcliff stopped in to lock up the house. I told him you were still out. He left the kitchen door open for you. He asks that you lock it when you get back.*

She'd forgotten that Mr. Radcliff said he locked up after dinner. She was tapping a quick reply to acknowledge James's message when headlights shone behind her. She locked her phone to turn off the screen's backlight and ducked down. The car rolled past, wheels crunching over the thin layer of ice. She peeked over the dash and saw a Jeep pull in behind Ingrid's car.

Maggie stayed low but kept an eye on the Jeep, willing the door to open and the driver to reveal himself. When the door finally groaned open, a tall man climbed out.

Craig Baldwin. She sank down before he saw her. She remembered Ingrid threatening to throw Craig out of her house. *This must be where he lives too.*

She listened until the sound of a door closing split the quiet, and then she popped up. She hated to think that she had just tailed two innocent people as they headed home from work and that the long, cold wait had been for nothing, but she suspected it was true. Still, she sat in the car until eight o'clock just in case. When there was still no movement, she returned to Weatherly Village, feeling a little silly. She parked in the lot next to the motor home and saw that its interior was dark and still. The women inside must have favored an early bedtime, given the busy day and the lateness of the previous night.

Maggie made sure the van was locked up tight and set off for the manor house. She had to climb over the gate, feeling foolish but left with no alternative. She didn't want to disturb the occupants of the motor home just to ask Lily for a key. As she dropped to the pavement on the other side of the fence, Maggie felt exhaustion flow into her limbs. She was eager to get to bed, but she knew that sleep would be hard to come by, what with her thoughts of Amanda's plight running through her mind. She wished she were back at Sedgwick Manor, where she'd let the stress of a hard day evaporate over a cup of tea and a cuddle with her cat, Snickers, but a young girl's life hung in the balance, and Maggie was a long way from home.

Her first step was to call Detective Adams and tell him about Ingrid and Craig's conversation. She pulled out her phone and continued to walk, watching her phone for a strong signal. The bars lit up near the schoolhouse, bringing her to a halt. Though it was getting late, she dialed.

The phone rang five times before going to voice mail. She left a message and stowed her phone before starting down the road again. As she approached the house, she had an odd feeling that someone was watching her, but she was sure there had been no headlights behind her when she pulled into the lot. She spun to look back the way she'd come. No shadowy figures or danger lurked behind; only a row of dark, empty shops and a few eddies of swirling snow greeted her.

"You're tired, and you're letting your imagination get the best of you," she told herself firmly, trying to draw comfort from her own voice. She started back down the road and through the yard to the manor's back door. She pulled it open and reveled in the toasty warmth from the cookstove. The room was lit by a gas lamp on the far side of the wall. She'd have to remember to thank Mr. Radcliff for leaving it burning for her.

She locked the door behind her and blew out the light, then went to the window to watch for anyone who had followed her. She stood there for a long moment but saw no movement outside.

"Imagination," she murmured, then headed down the hallway to the sitting room. The manor was eerily quiet; her friends must have retired to their rooms already. She followed the warm glow of light spilling from the sitting room into the hallway. She entered the room to find James sitting on the sofa in the lamplight, an architecture book in his lap. She felt a pang of guilt for keeping him up waiting to see her home safely, but she took a moment to thank God for putting such a caring friend in her life.

He looked up, and she was struck by how handsome he looked in the flickering light of the Clambroth Glass oil lamp. "Well well, if my wayward wife hasn't finally found her way home."

Maggie grinned at his comment, glad that he wouldn't see her blushing in the dim light. "My dear sir," she said formally, "it was kind of you to wait up for me."

"My pleasure, madam." He stood and stretched, breaking character with a decidedly informal yawn. "Did you discover anything interesting?"

"No."

"Then if it's all the same to you, I'm going to turn in."

"I'm really sorry to have kept you up. You should have been in bed already."

"It was the gentlemanly thing to do, and I am nothing if not the gentleman of the estate." He picked up the lamp. "Shall I walk you to your room?"

"I think I'll make a cup of tea to warm up and settle my nerves a bit."

He handed the lamp to her. "I can find my way without this."

"Seriously, James. Thank you for waiting up. I appreciate knowing that you were watching out for me."

"Anytime," he said, and she knew he was being sincere.

She held the light for him as he climbed the stairs, then made her way down the hallway to the kitchen. She set the lamp on the island and moved to the glowing stove where a copper teakettle sat, but the rustic brick wall caught her attention.

With everyone in bed and most of the staff gone for the night, it was the perfect time to check out the secret stairway to see where it led.

She located the correct brick, pressed, and the door swung open. With her cell phone flashlight, she crept into the opening. She climbed the stairs steadily, holding fast to the railing as she went. The thought of falling in a secret passageway where only the Baldwins might discover her made her stomach churn with anxiety.

Midway up the railing, her hand encountered something sticky. Not knowing what it might be, she jerked her hand free, the stickiness lingering when she prodded her palm with her fingers. She bent forward and studied the rail. What appeared to be tape residue circled the railing where she'd grasped it. *Odd.*

She filed it in the back of her mind and then shined her light ahead. The beam landed on a door at the top of the stairs.

She made her way to the top and pushed open the door. A blast of cold air rushed in.

The door led outside. *How strange.*

She shined the light through the opening to discover a crumbling rooftop deck on a flat portion of the roof in the rear section of the house.

She crossed the deck and made her way to a dilapidated railing. Careful not to lean on the rotting wood, she peered over the edge. A shadow on the ground below moved, the shape of it clearer for a moment before it darted out of sight along the wall of the house. It was a person. Someone was prowling around outside the house.

Had someone followed her after all, leaving distance between them in the same way she'd tailed Ingrid? It certainly was possible.

Her heart rate kicked up.

A gust of wind blew over the roof, catching her off-balance. She lurched back and fell hard on the deck. At the same moment, the wind caught the door, slamming it closed with a deafening finality.

"Please don't be locked!" she cried. She jolted to her feet, rubbing her elbow where she'd landed. She grabbed the handle and tugged. It didn't budge. She pulled harder. The door remained closed.

Oh no.

She was locked out, stuck high on the roof in freezing temperatures.

She checked her phone for a signal and found only one bar, blinking feebly in and out of existence. She crept around the rooftop, looking for a better signal. When she found none, she tried to dial James anyway, but the call failed. If she texted, there was no way to know if anyone would receive it before morning. Still, she took off her mittens and thumbed in a message to all of her friends staying in the manor. She added Daisy as well, banking on the marginally better cell service at the motor home.

I'm stuck on the roof. There's a hidden door in the kitchen by the stove. If it's closed, press on the bricks until you find the loose one and push hard. Please reply if you get this text.

It appeared to have gone through, but all her friends were asleep, and she had no way to know whether their phones would awaken them if they got her message. Panic settled in.

She had to find a way off the roof, but how?

Maybe she could alert someone in the house. She looked around until she saw a loose board and freed it from the support. Hoping to make enough noise to wake the person in the room located directly below, she lifted the wood high and pounded on the crumbling deck. She bashed the board into the deck over and over until she was exhausted, then listened for sounds of someone coming to her rescue.

Silence reigned—there was no sound in the stillness but her own ragged breathing.

Even if the person below had heard her, how would he or she find her? As far as she could tell there was only one point of access to the roof, and her rescuer would either have to find or know about the secret entrance in the kitchen to use it. As far as she knew, the only ones aware of that passageway were Craig and Ingrid. Not a comforting thought.

She resumed pounding and waiting alternately until she determined she was wasting her energy. On the bright side, the physical labor kept her warm, and she was burning off the calories from the cake with whipped cream she'd had for dessert. *Small comfort if I'm not rescued soon.*

She dropped the board and returned to the railing to look over the side again. The figure was gone, and she caught sight of a light burning in Oliver's cottage. He might be up and would be able to see her from his window. She turned on the flashlight app on her phone and waved it in the air.

Her arm soon tired, but at least the movement had kept her blood flowing, a necessary pursuit if she was to survive the bitter cold. Despair started to close in around Maggie, and her thoughts turned to Amanda and to her own daughter. *Lord, keep them both safe.*

The door to the secret stairwell suddenly opened, and her heart lurched with relief. She moved toward the door, but a man stood in the shadows and didn't step out.

She stilled her feet.

"James? Is that you?" she asked.

He didn't respond.

With a sinking feeling, Maggie realized that rescue might be the last thing on this person's mind. Had she just signaled the prowler—or worse, the person responsible for Amanda's disappearance? She fought the urge to scream as the man slowly emerged into the pale moonlight.

"**M**s. Watson, is that you?"

Maggie recognized the voice, and her shoulders sagged with relief. "Mr. Dorn?"

"Yes ma'am," he replied. "I saw your light from the cottage and thought someone was in trouble. Then on my way up to the manor, I saw someone sneaking around the house and thought he could be the one doing the signaling. What with all the funny business around here lately, I figured I best check it out."

"Thank goodness you did." She made her way across the deck, careful not to trip on the warped and broken lumber. "I saw someone sneaking around too."

"So I didn't imagine it then." He frowned. "Not a good thing, I tell you. I reckon you're glad not to spend the night out here."

"Very much so. And I'm glad to have you answer the door instead of someone out to do me harm."

"How did you get up here, anyway?"

"I went to the kitchen to make a cup of tea and . . ." She trailed off with a shrug, hesitant to tell anyone who didn't need to know how she'd previously discovered the stairwell.

Oliver gestured into the dark space. "I've been pestering Donald to seal off this passage, but he plans to rebuild the deck so people who stay at the house can use it in the summer. He figures if we have a secret passage and a rooftop deck, we can charge more for the weekend stays."

"It doesn't sound like you think that's a good idea."

"I'd rather not have any more people staying here, but Donald's all about the money, and he won't hear a word against it."

Another gust of wind blew across the flat roof and whistled against the wall. Maggie shivered, not only from the frosty air, but from her lingering fears.

Oliver gestured at the stairway again. "Let's get you out of the cold."

For a brief moment, Maggie hesitated. She believed Oliver to be a good person, but she didn't really know him, and she wasn't sure if she should go into a hidden passageway with him.

He must have sensed her hesitation. "There's an entrance in the stairwell for each floor. Wait here and I'll get the door to the second floor open for you." He disappeared down the stairway. She heard him fumble around and then light flooded into the stairs.

"Hello?" she heard James call out. "Who's been pounding?"

At the comforting sound of James's voice, Maggie started down the stairs and entered the second-floor hallway. She blinked to let her eyes adjust to the lamp he held high.

"Maggie? What in the world?"

"She got stuck on the roof," Oliver said. "I saw her distress signal."

"And came to my rescue." Maggie introduced Oliver, and then she told James about her adventure in the stairwell, making sure to shoot him a look urging him to keep quiet about the conversation she'd overheard earlier.

James furrowed his brow. "If the two of you really did see someone lurking outside, we should check the house to make sure everyone is safe."

"I came in through the front door, and it was still locked," Oliver said. "I didn't check the kitchen door."

"Then let's do that now," Maggie said.

In the foyer, Oliver lit a lamp for Maggie. She'd never wished for electric lights more than at that moment. The idea of searching for an intruder in a darkened old house made her skin crawl.

They made their way slowly and silently through the first level of the house. As they entered the kitchen, the memory of being stuck on the roof came flooding back, causing Maggie to shiver. James eyed her but didn't comment. Still, she knew he was concerned for her safety.

Oliver went to the door. "It's ajar."

"I'm positive I locked it," Maggie said.

Oliver pulled it open and shined his light on the wood that was splintered and fractured. "It's been jimmied open."

Maggie's heart skipped a beat. "So someone did come inside."

"And could still be here," James warned. "We need to finish checking all of the rooms."

"Or it might be better to call the sheriff's office and have a deputy dispatched," Oliver said. "We've had a bit of trouble with vandalism in the past, and I wouldn't want to trample over any evidence."

"Do you think this could be related to Amanda's disappearance?" Maggie asked.

"There's no way to know."

"We should listen to Oliver and call in a deputy," James said.

Oliver faced Maggie. "I don't have a cell phone. Could you make the call?"

She put her lamp on the counter and got out her phone. "No signal." She fought back panic, wishing she could dash upstairs to check on her friends, but she knew that the authorities should be contacted immediately.

"Donald's office has the only landline in the village," Oliver said. "I have keys and can run over there to call."

Maggie felt a combination of appreciation and relief flood through her. "That will give us a chance to look in on our friends to be sure they're all right too."

Oliver met her gaze. "Be careful."

"We will." James held out his hand for Maggie. "After you."

She didn't need to be told twice. With lamp in hand, she hurried down the hall to the main staircase. There she found Ruth, Ina, and June standing at the second-floor landing.

"I was just coming to check on you all," Maggie called to them. "I'm glad you're all okay."

Ruth arched an eyebrow. "Is there a reason we shouldn't be?"

Ina stifled a yawn. "Does this have to do with the banging we heard?"

Maggie explained about being locked on the roof and about the intruder. "The caretaker has gone to Mr. Radcliff's office to call the police."

June's eyes widened. "Do you think we're in danger?"

"I'm sure we aren't. But until the police can search the upstairs, I suggest we all wait in the sitting room."

Ruth tightened the belt on her robe and started down the steps. "Who do you think could have broken in?"

"Oliver said they've had some problems with vandalism," James offered.

"But that seems odd to me." Maggie led the way toward the sitting room. "In the winter, the village is closed during the week. So why wait until there are people around to vandalize the place?"

"Good point." June raked her fingers through her hair, settling mussed-up strands in place. "Do you think the break-in is related to Amanda's disappearance, then?"

"I think it has to be." Maggie went to the window overlooking Main Street to watch for Oliver and the deputy.

She heard the floorboards creak behind her and turned to see her friends taking a seat. They probably had the right idea, but even if Maggie didn't want to see the deputy the minute he arrived, she was too worked up from the night's events to sit. James lit a few lamps, casting out the dark shadows, but Maggie gazed out the window until Oliver came out of Mr. Radcliff's office. She rushed to the door and waited for him on the porch.

When Oliver caught sight of her, he picked up speed. "Deputy Matthews will be here momentarily. We're in his patrol area, and he's just down the road."

"Perfect. Thank you."

"And your friends?" He climbed the stairs.

"They're fine and waiting in the sitting room for the deputy to arrive and clear the house. Would you like to wait with us?"

"I don't want to intrude."

"You won't be." She opened the door, and after he entered, she locked it behind him. In the sitting room, she introduced him to the women and then returned to the window.

"Watching won't bring the deputy here any faster," James said.

"I'm with you, Ms. Watson." Oliver joined her at the window. "I don't much like the idea of a criminal strolling through our property, and the waiting is about killing me."

She turned. "Please, call me Maggie, okay?"

"If that's what you'd like."

"It is."

"In that case, I'm Oliver." He ran a hand through his hair, leaving little tufts standing up. "I don't often interact with our visitors, but if they were all as nice as you, I might start."

"What a kind thing to say."

"Wouldn't say it if it wasn't true."

Maggie smiled at him, then resumed her watch out the window. The ladies and James chatted about their plans for the next day, but she couldn't think beyond the deputy arriving and tuned them out as her mind whirred with the possible reasons someone would break in the manor house in the dead of night.

If she hadn't found herself locked on the roof and hadn't made a ruckus, there was no telling what the prowler might have done. She glanced at the wall clock and kept taking quick peeks at it. Five long minutes passed before Deputy Matthews strode up the street.

Maggie hurried to the door, followed closely by Oliver. She pulled it open and went to meet the deputy.

"Is everyone inside okay and accounted for?" he asked.

"Yes," Maggie said. "We're all in the sitting room, waiting for you to clear the house so we can go to bed."

"It's likely that if there was an intruder, he's already fled the scene, but I'd like you both to stay with the group while I check out the house."

The three of them stepped inside, and the deputy lifted his gun from his holster and headed straight up the stairs.

"He took out his gun," Oliver whispered. Maggie was surprised by how pale and worried the old man looked, and her heart went out to him.

"He has to protect himself. I'm sure it's just a precaution," Maggie murmured calmly, though seeing the weapon had unsettled her too. "I'd appreciate it if you didn't mention it to the ladies. I don't want to worry them."

He agreed, and they rejoined the group.

"Deputy Matthews is upstairs right now, checking the bedrooms," Maggie said, keeping her voice light to ease her friends' worry.

Ina sighed and leaned back on the sofa. "All of this excitement has tuckered me out."

Ruth took Ina's hand. "I'm sure the deputy will be finished in no time, and we can go back to bed."

"Good," Ina said. "I need to get my sleep if I'm going to stay up for game night tomorrow."

"Speaking of games, I saw a checkerboard and cribbage game in the library this afternoon," June said. "Fair warning: I'm a master at checkers and plan to be crowned champion tomorrow night."

The ladies started a playful argument about who was the best checkers player in the room.

Deputy Matthews poked his head into the room, and Maggie was grateful to see he'd holstered his gun. "The upstairs is clear. I'll check this floor and be back in a jiffy."

"Thank you," Maggie said, her mind going back to the roof and the man lurking in the shadows.

Since she didn't believe this was a case of a simple break-in, she wondered if Craig or Ingrid had come back to the manor for some reason. But she didn't want to alert Oliver to Craig and Ingrid's secret. Maggie trusted the caretaker, but she was sure that the more people who knew, the greater the chances the news would travel around the village, ruining her ability to properly look into the pair and their mysterious plan. And she felt it was premature to worry her friends over something she knew so little about.

The discussion had returned to the games, and it wasn't long before Deputy Matthews came back. "I found nothing amiss except the damage to the kitchen door."

"Did you check every room?" Oliver asked.

"Yes, and they're all clear. Presumably, the intruder planned to steal something of value, so it would be a good idea to take inventory of the valuables in the house. Are you familiar with the antiques or do we need to call Mr. Radcliff to come out?" the deputy asked Oliver.

"I spend enough time working in here, and I know the pieces as well as he does, though he'll want to do an inventory himself in the morning."

Deputy Matthews addressed the rest of the group. "You all should check your rooms for missing items as well."

"You mean this thief could have come in while we were asleep?" Ina asked, indignation in every line of her face.

Maggie hated to see her friend so upset, although she imagined any intruder who tried to sneak past Ina would come off worse for it. "I highly doubt it."

"Would it help if we stayed together for the search of your room?" June asked.

"Yes, thank you. But I'm warning you, if we come across any stranger lurking in a closet, I'll use my butter-churning muscles to give him what for!" Ina replied, brandishing her small fists like a prizefighter.

James came to his feet, chuckling at Ina's spunky response to the situation. "Let's get to it so we can catch at least a few hours of sleep tonight."

"I'll type up my report here. If you need me, just holler," the deputy said.

"I'll accompany you all upstairs and check the antiques so you can get to bed," Oliver said and led the way up the stairs.

He went into Ina's room first and took a quick trip around the perimeter. "Everything's here." He shot what looked like an admiring glance at Ina, and Maggie wondered if it was as obvious to her friend as it was to her. "Don't worry, ma'am. I'll be securing that kitchen door before I leave, and you'll all be safe and sound."

"Thank you," Ina said, her ready smile returning.

"Will you be okay alone now?" Maggie asked.

"Yes. I might be putting a chair under the knob, though." Her grin morphed into a chuckle.

Maggie gave Ina a hug, then bid her good night.

"I think we can split up now, and Oliver can make his way around the other rooms," Maggie said.

The others agreed, and Maggie crossed the hall to her room, moving first to the dresser to check her belongings. She found nothing missing from her purse and wallet and was turning to check the armoire when she noticed something sticking out from under her pillow.

"Did you find something?" James asked from the doorway, startling her.

"There's something under my pillow." She shined her lamp over the bed. "It's a piece of paper."

She tugged the paper free, unfolded it, and held it up to the lamp for a better look. It was a color photo printed on plain white paper. She examined it closer and gasped.

"What in the world—?" she managed to get out, before dropping both the picture and the lamp to the floor in shock.

It was a picture of Amanda.

12

"**W**hat is it?" James darted forward to catch her lamp before it broke and set it gently on the bedside table.

Maggie's mind whirled to make sense of what she'd seen, and she couldn't form any words.

James stooped as if planning to pick up the picture.

Maggie grabbed a tissue from the nightstand. "Use this to touch it."

He lifted the paper and glanced at it. "Amanda, I take it?" His voice was grim.

"I'm afraid so." Maggie forced herself to study the photograph, which looked like it had been converted from digital format using an ink-jet printer. Amanda was sitting in a wooden armchair, her arms tied, her mouth gagged. Tearstains covered her face, and she looked dirty but unharmed. A time stamp of only a few hours earlier was visible in the lower right corner.

A typed note on the bottom of the page read, *Amanda is alive . . . for now. I'll release her soon if no one gets in my way.*

"She's alive, and he says he'll let her go. I wonder what he means by no one getting in his way. Do you think he has accomplices who might be giving him a hard time, or is he referring to the police? Or could he mean . . . *me*?" She gulped.

"Could be any or all of the above." James's eyes narrowed. "Or maybe he wants to strike fear into our hearts so it paralyzes us."

"Well if that's the case, the fear part is working, but we can't be paralyzed." Maggie took the picture from James and stared at it. "There must be something here to give us a hint as to where he's hiding her."

James moved closer. "What about the wall behind her or the chair?"

Maggie studied the rough wooden wall and noted that Amanda sat in an ordinary oak chair. "They're both so generic. I would think in this rural community there are plenty of rustic walls and simple oak chairs like this one, so it doesn't narrow things down at all. And there's nothing else in the picture."

She pointed at a greenish streak running down the middle of the picture. "Do you think the printer that was used to print this is malfunctioning?"

"Could be a leaky ink-jet or something on the print roller."

"So if I find this printer, I could find the person who is holding Amanda captive."

"It won't be easy, though. Most people have them in their homes these days, or the printer could be in a public area like the library or an office where anyone could have used it."

"I suppose the best way to start is with the people on my list of suspects, like Kyle, Ingrid, or Craig. I'll check to see if any of them have access to a printer on the premises. Then I should also check Mr. Radcliff's office."

"What about a printshop in town?"

She raised an eyebrow. "I doubt they'd have a printer that leaves streaks, or people wouldn't pay for the prints."

"That's true," he admitted.

Oliver poked his head in the doorway, and Maggie quickly folded the paper out of sight.

"Did you notice anything missing?" he asked.

"Nothing obvious."

Oliver frowned. "This is my last room up here. So far, nothing appears to be missing."

"Perhaps we scared off the intruder before he could take anything," Maggie suggested.

"Hello?" Deputy Matthews called out from below.

Oliver spun toward the door. "I'll go finish searching the downstairs and talk to the deputy."

"Thank you, Oliver." Maggie smiled, but let it fall the minute he left the room.

"You're planning to tell the deputy about the note, right?" James asked.

"Right now, actually."

They left her room and found the deputy and Oliver in the foyer.

"I'll finish my search," Oliver told the deputy. "And if it's okay I'd like to secure the kitchen door."

"Sounds good."

Oliver glanced up at Maggie and James. "Good night to you both."

"Good night," Maggie said, and when he'd disappeared down the hallway she held the picture at the corner with a tissue and displayed it for the deputy. "I found this under my pillow."

He studied it. "Detective Adams needs to see this. I'll retrieve an evidence bag from my car and arrange to have him dispatched. Until then, don't let anyone else touch the paper."

"I'll wait in the sitting room." Maggie took a seat on the sofa and laid the picture on the cushion next to her.

James joined her, sitting on the far cushion.

She smiled at him. "I appreciate your support, but you should get some sleep. I'll be fine on my own."

"I'll wait." His tone brooked no argument. "Is there anything I can do to help find Amanda?"

She pondered his question and mentally reviewed the things she had to do in the morning, but they jumbled together in a tangled mess in her brain so all she could think about was the photo. "It seems like the green streak on the picture is a good place to start, so you could check in with Mr. Radcliff to see if he has an ink-jet printer or if there are other printers in the village. If so, you could have him print a sample page to look for the streak."

"I'll try that. I can also check the library in town if you think the suspect might have used the printer there."

"Good idea. If the person who left the picture is smart, they wouldn't use their own printer."

"That makes sense."

Maggie's thoughts continued to race through her head. "At this point, I still think Ingrid, Craig, and Kyle are my top suspects. So the question is, which one of them might have been sneaking around here tonight?"

"It would make sense with Ingrid working late on these special weekends that she has a key to the kitchen. If she does, she wouldn't need to break down the door. Maybe we could rule her and Craig out, since he would probably have access to her key."

"Even if she has a key, she seems like a smart cookie, and she might have broken the door to keep the police from looking at her."

"True. So we can't really rule out her or Craig."

"Exactly." Maggie stared at the picture. "I need to snap a photo of this page for reference before the deputy takes it away."

She used the tissue to unfold the paper and then took several shots with her cell phone camera. "My head is starting to spin with everything I learned today. I need to jot it down in my notebook to make sense of it all."

"We could do that now if you like."

"I'll run up to my room to get it." She charged up the stairs, trusting James to keep an eye on the picture.

By the time she returned with notebook in hand, Deputy Matthews had returned and was putting the picture in an evidence bag.

He looked up. "Adams is on his way."

"Are you taking the picture with you?"

"No," he replied. "Adams instructed me to remain on site until he gets here to take it into evidence."

If Maggie hadn't seen her share of TV crime shows, she might not have recognized that the deputy was following evidence chain-of-custody procedures, and she might have thought he didn't trust her. "Feel free to have a seat while you wait."

"Actually, I think I'll take another look around the main floor." Holding the bag, he left the room.

Maggie took her place on the sofa and opened her notebook. She jotted SUSPECTS on the top of a blank page, then listed each person of interest below. Next to each name, she noted possible motives for holding Amanda hostage. Kyle's list was far longer than the others.

She showed the list to James. "I should have made time today to question the town blacksmith, Gabe Hendricks. I'll have to rectify that tomorrow."

She flipped the page and wrote PICTURE, then noted *printer streak* and *printer access*? under the heading. Below she added a list of different locations to check.

"I'll mark your name by Mr. Radcliff's office and the library. If Mr. Radcliff's printer produces the streak, be sure to ask him about other people who have access to the printer."

"Don't worry," James said. "I can handle this."

"I know. Forgive me. I'm still a little rattled. Have I mentioned recently how grateful I am for your help?" Maggie looked up in time to see him flash her an encouraging smile before turning her attention back to her lists. She tapped the end of her pen on the notebook. "You could also ask Mr. Radcliff if anyone else has a key to this house. Not that it will help us figure out who might have broken in, but we might find it important later on."

"Good idea."

"Oh, and can you also ask if he's learned anything about the missing money?"

"Yes."

She scribbled a reminder on the page to follow up with James on that specific item.

A knock sounded on the front door.

"That will be the detective." Maggie stood. "Would you mind telling the deputy that the detective is here?"

"Glad to." James disappeared down the hallway while Maggie went to answer the door.

Detective Adams stood on the porch, his hand running over his head as he glanced around. He looked tired and overworked.

Maggie offered a sympathetic smile. "Any word or updates on your search for Amanda?"

"No." He snapped on latex gloves. "You have a picture for me?"

"The deputy has it. My friend James is getting him."

The detective ran his fingers over the lock. "I take it this isn't the door that was breached."

"No, it was the kitchen door." She moved out of the way to let the detective into the house.

Maggie heard footsteps in the hall, and Deputy Matthews and James joined them. Detective Adams held out his hand for the evidence bag.

He glanced at Maggie. "I suppose your prints are all over this."

"Unfortunately, I did pick it up from my bed and open it before I knew what it was. But since I realized it was evidence, I've used a tissue to touch it."

He opened the paper and stared at it for a few moments. When he looked up, a scowl drew down his mouth.

"A picture showing Amanda alive is a good sign, right?" she asked.

"Good? I caution against jumping to any conclusions, ma'am. We have no way of knowing if the time stamp was altered or if something has happened to her in the meantime."

"Still, the captor says she's alive for now, and he's going to release her. And he's not making any demands, so . . ." Maggie trailed off, a sudden realization coming to her. "Do you think Amanda's kidnapping was unplanned, like a spur-of-the-moment thing? Maybe she saw something she shouldn't have, and he didn't want her to tell anyone."

Deputy Matthews cleared his throat. "It's clear now that she wasn't taken for ransom, but there are many other possible motives for abduction."

Maggie's heart sank, but she couldn't fault his logic. "Speaking of motives, I talked to Kyle's mother. She said he didn't come home straight from work as he'd told me. He was out very late, and she had no idea where he'd gone. She's been worried about him."

Detective Adams slid the picture back into the bag. "If that's all, I'll grab my fingerprint kit from the car. I'll process your room when I come back." He and the deputy walked outside.

"That didn't help us find Amanda," Maggie said.

"But it could have helped the detective. We've got professionals on the case, and they'll get Amanda home safe and sound. We need to have faith," James reminded her gently.

"You're right," Maggie said. "I'll keep praying for Amanda's safety, but in the morning, I hope we can find some answers to all of these questions."

Because I can't help but fear that Amanda is running out of time.

13

"What do you mean Amanda might be *here*? On the property?" Maggie laid her fork on her empty breakfast plate and stared at June in disbelief.

Dressed in a gingham gown and bonnet, June sat across the breakfast table from Maggie. Ruth, James, and Ina, also dressed in their costumes, all stopped midbite to look at June expectantly. That morning, the breakfast buffet was piled high with fluffy scrambled eggs from chickens raised on the property, freshly ground sausages, homemade buttery biscuits, and hot oatmeal.

June wiped her mouth with a cloth napkin. "In the picture of Amanda, the wall behind her is rustic, and there are plenty of rustic walls in the buildings on this property."

"Plus no one saw her leave Weatherly Village." Ruth set down her coffee cup. "And since there were no snowmobile or other tracks, her abductor would have had to take her down Main Street to move her off the property. He'd have been seen if he'd done so."

"True," Maggie said, thinking it over. "At least, it sounds possible to me that she would have been held here until everyone went home. But I think there are too many people around the village to risk keeping Amanda here for long."

"Or if she *is* here, there's a secret hiding place that no one else knows about," Ruth added.

Maggie thought of the secret stairway, but she already knew firsthand that Amanda wasn't being held there.

"I think it's more likely that he did what Ruth said," June replied. "Hid her here, and then moved her later. But we should all keep our eyes open for a similar rustic wall when we wander the village today in case that's where he took the picture."

The others murmured their agreement.

"Thank you," Maggie said. "That would be wonderful. Let me know if you see anything that matches."

She turned to Daisy. "How are Jasmine and Lily holding up this morning?"

"They're doing well, but Amanda's mother is a wreck, so Jasmine has been on the phone with her regularly to offer her support. Well, as regularly as she can be with the reception out here. On the bright side, though, it sounds like Amanda's mother finally found a flight home. So there's that to be thankful for." Tears glistened in Daisy's eyes, and Maggie felt her own tearing up for the poor woman.

"We all need to keep praying for her and Amanda," Ina said firmly.

"Amen to that," Ruth said.

"Now, I really need to get going." Maggie rose to move her dishes onto the empty tray on the sideboard.

James joined her. "Where are you going in such a hurry?"

"I want to catch Kyle and Craig before the town fills up with visitors. I need to ask about their alibis for last night."

"I'm going to talk to Mr. Radcliff about the printer, so I'll walk out with you."

In the sitting room where they'd left their coats, James held out the warm wool coat for her and settled it on her shoulders. She thanked him, then carefully navigated the porch steps to avoid getting hung up in the voluminous skirt.

They crossed the street where vendors had set up small carts and tables loaded with their wares.

"I still need to find time to get to the antique dealers' booths," she said wistfully as they passed one loaded with beautiful authentic pieces. "June has already checked them out and bought items for the shop, but I still want to browse."

"Why don't we set a time to meet here later? That might be the only way to guarantee you'll take a break from sleuthing long enough to enjoy yourself a little." His blue-gray eyes sparkled at her.

"You don't think I'll stand you up, huh?"

"Why, Mrs. Weatherly, I know you exceedingly well. My dear wife would never miss a stroll about town with her doting husband." He linked arms with her, and they ambled together to the sidewalk outside Mr. Radcliff's office, smiling at the arriving villagers as they went.

James released her arm and faced her. "After getting that picture last night, we can assume whoever has Amanda knows who you are, so be careful today, okay?"

"I will. How about we meet at this vendor right after this morning's game?"

"It's a date." He walked through the door to Mr. Radcliff's office, leaving her blushing like a schoolgirl over the word *date*.

At the inn, she found Craig behind the counter and Lily scooping ashes from the fireplace. Lily had most likely seen all of the rooms at the inn during her training, and she'd know of any walls that matched the one in the photo. Maggie approached her first, leaving the more difficult confrontation with Craig for later.

"You look like you're working hard," Maggie said kindly.

"Mom says someone left a picture of Amanda on your bed." The words rushed out of Lily's mouth. "That's good, right? I mean, it tells us she's alive."

"In my opinion, it's very good," Maggie replied. She decided not to downplay the positive implications of the photo as Detective Adams had done last night. Lily needed all the positivity she could muster to cope with her friend's disappearance.

Maggie chose not to display the picture for Lily, thinking it would upset her to see Amanda gagged and tied up, so she opted to describe the wall instead. "It's possible Amanda's still in the village. Have you seen any unfinished walls here at the inn, or heard of any secret places or storage areas that might be overlooked?"

The girl frowned, clearly thinking it over. "I can't think of any secret places where someone could be hidden, and all the walls here are plaster except . . . wait." She moved closer. "There are a few rooms upstairs that I haven't seen. Craig said they aren't open to the public because they haven't been restored, so he didn't bother to take us through them."

Maggie's excitement mounted upon learning of a potential hiding place that only Craig had access to. "Could you show them to me?"

"Sure, but Craig is watching us, so I'm going to say something to throw him off." She raised her voice until she was nearly shouting at Maggie. "The bedrooms? Yes ma'am, they're open for viewing. Why don't I take you upstairs and answer any questions you might have?"

Maggie grinned at Lily's playacting. "That's most helpful. Thank you so much," she replied, matching Lily's volume.

Lily set her pail and shovel in a small alcove, then led the way past a small dining room. Maggie spotted a fire crackling merrily in the dining room hearth and a rustic pot bubbling over the fire. Something smelled of garlic, and a sign announced today's lunch was beef stew and crusty bread.

They passed four bedrooms with ropes strung across their thresholds. Maggie slowed to take them in and caught sight of colorful quilts and big four-poster beds. She stopped to admire a primitive armoire with hand-painted doors that displayed blue ribbons and pink bows on a tan background.

"The unfinished rooms are down here," Lily said as she unhooked a rope cordoning off the end of the hallway.

Maggie slipped by her, then waited for Lily to return the rope to the hook and open the first door. It groaned open and a musty smell filled Maggie's nostrils. They crept inside. The original architectural details had survived in this room, including the pumpkin pine floors and paneled wainscoting, but the upper plaster walls were water stained. Furniture was piled high, and the bed was covered with a dusty sheet.

"These walls aren't like the ones you described," Lily said.

"No they're not. Let's move on to the other room."

They crossed the hall, and Lily had to put her shoulder to the next door to get it to open. Inside, they found a room similar in size to the first one, except the ceiling plaster had fallen and covered the water-damaged wood floors. A solid walnut rocking chair coated with a thick layer of dust sat in the corner. It had a carved crown on top, burl walnut trim, and Victorian incising on the arms. Maggie wanted to clean it up and display it on the property so people could appreciate it, or take it back to Somerset Harbor with her so she and June could find it a good home.

"Dang," Lily said. "The walls might be in bad shape, but they're plaster, not wood."

"How about an attic?" Maggie asked. "Do you know if there is one?"

"We don't have an attic." Craig's voice came from behind, making them both jump.

Maggie took a breath and turned to face him, but he had his gaze pinned on Lily. "What are you doing, showing her this room?"

She twisted her hands. "She wanted to see all of the rooms."

"They're off-limits for the guests."

"Maggie's a friend of my aunt's, so I didn't think it would hurt."

He met Maggie's gaze. "And did you find what you were looking for?"

"Actually, no," Maggie said truthfully. "But I'm sure you've heard about the break-in at the manor last night."

He held up a hand. "Before you ask, I was at home with my stepmother all night. She's the cook at the manor house. You can ask her, and she'll vouch for me."

If Maggie hadn't overheard their conversation in the stairwell, she would have considered this a solid alibi for the break-in, but the pair were up to something, and Craig's ongoing adversarial attitude helped cement that thought in Maggie's mind.

Still, there was no point in asking Ingrid if Craig had been with her. Even if he hadn't been at home, Ingrid was sure to lie to protect her stepson.

"Have you heard anything else about Amanda?" Maggie asked.

"No," he said sulkily.

"Would you tell me if you had?"

"Look, lady." He crossed his arms. "I have no idea where Amanda is, so lay off before I ask Donald to kick you off the property."

"I'm not trying to offend you," Maggie replied honestly. "I just want to see Amanda returned home safe and sound. Don't you want that too?"

His gaze softened. "Yes," he said quietly. It was the first sincere expression of concern for Amanda that he'd demonstrated.

"If you know anything about her that could help, now would be a good time to tell me."

He sighed. "Like I said, I don't know where she is."

Maggie could tell by his tone of voice that she was wasting her time pressing him further. "If you hear anything, will you let me know?"

He gave a clipped nod, then gestured at the hallway. "It's time for you both to go back downstairs."

They scurried ahead of him, and Maggie heard the metal end of the rope clip into the clasp.

"I didn't get you in trouble, did I?" Maggie asked.

"It doesn't matter if you did." Lily squared her shoulders. "I'd get in all the trouble in the world if it brought Amanda home."

"I know you would, honey." Maggie stopped in the lobby. "After the break-in last night, there's bound to be gossip. If you hear anything that you think I should know, please find me."

"Sure." A small smile found Lily's lips. "Thank you for all you're doing to help find her."

"I'm glad to do it." Maggie squeezed Lily's arm and headed for the door. She checked the time and knew she had to hurry if she was going to talk to Kyle and still get back in time for the Game of Graces demonstration. She considered putting it off until after the game, but she didn't want him to have additional time to come up with an alibi for last night. She'd also agreed to spend time with James and didn't want to miss her chance to browse the vendor market before they left town tomorrow.

She was thankful to find the door to the haymow open. Kyle was forking hay onto a small wagon. Flakes of hay and dust were captured by the bright sunshine as they flitted into the air. The dust made her sneeze.

Kyle looked up, and suspicion darkened his gaze. "What do you want now?"

He'd started out with an attitude, so there was no point in beating around the bush. "Where were you last night between nine thirty and eleven o'clock?"

He rested the fork against the wagon and crossed his arms over a worn cotton work jacket. "Home with my mom."

"The same place you claimed to be on Thursday night?"

He scowled. "My mom told me you talked to her."

"Then you know she told me you weren't home until much later than you told me you were. How can you account for that time?"

His arms tightened. "I don't have to tell you where I was. You're not the police."

"No, but the detective was definitely interested when I mentioned that you lied about your alibi. I'm sure he'll want to take you in for questioning."

"Then I'll deal with that if it happens." He grabbed the pitchfork and shoved it into a pile of hay, effectively dismissing her.

Maggie needed to call his mother to check on this latest alibi, but she didn't have any way to contact Hannah, so she stopped by Mr. Radcliff's office to look at his phone book.

While she flipped pages, he pulled out his pocket watch. "You best hurry. It's time for the Game of Graces. Mrs. Kaufman is leading today, and she doesn't abide tardiness."

"I know." Maggie chuckled. "I've already learned that firsthand."

"Have you?" He offered another of his strained smiles. "She can be a real taskmaster, but teachers back in the day were often very stern. Children certainly weren't coddled like the teens I work with here."

Maggie was again struck by his apparent dislike of young people, but she avoided further discussion by jotting down Hannah's number and making a hasty retreat. Despite the big skirt and tight shoes, she reached the side yard just as Mrs. Kaufman was clapping her hands to gain the attention of the talkative group. Tammy and another scullery maid stood off to the side holding wood rods and rings.

Maggie stopped next to James.

"I thought you were going to ditch us," he said.

"No, just running a bit late."

"Anything new?" he asked.

"Ladies and gentleman," Mrs. Kaufman said, giving James

her formidable glare. "It's time to listen. Let me tell you about the Game of Graces. It was considered a proper game benefiting young ladies, and it was also said that it was designed to make them more graceful." She looked at James again. "Though traditionally played by women and girls, the game is played in pairs, so we will need you to participate, Mr. Weatherly. I feel it's only proper that you do so with your wife."

James grinned at Maggie. "I'm more than happy to pair up with Mrs. Weatherly."

Mrs. Kaufmann turned to the others. "The rest of you choose a partner, and the maids will hand out your rods and rings."

June and Ina paired off, as did Ruth and Daisy. The maids handed two rods to each person and gave one person in each pair a ten-inch ring.

"Please face each other and put several feet between you," Mrs. Kaufman said. "The person with the ring, place it over your rods."

As the one with the ring, Maggie followed directions clumsily, feeling a little silly as the rods clacked loudly against the ring in her fumbling hands.

"Now hold the rods horizontally in front of you," Mrs. Kaufman continued, "and cross them in an X to keep the ring from sliding free."

Maggie let the ring slide slightly down the rod, and it fell off.

"I'm so glad you got the ring first," James said, a smile in his tone as he picked it up for her.

"Obviously you weren't paying attention," Mrs. Kaufman said acidly as she strode across the yard and adjusted Maggie's arms. "Now, partners, please stand with your rods facing up. When I signal, the person with the ring will jerk their rods apart. If done correctly, the ring will quickly slide up and shoot away toward your partner, who will catch the ring on their rods. Then the partner will send the ring back."

James lifted his rods, and Maggie waited for the signal.

Mrs. Kaufman stood back. "Let's begin with a few practice rounds, and then I'll evaluate your form. Ready? Go!"

Maggie snapped her rods apart and the ring went flying. Unfortunately, it shot over James's head and into the slushy snow.

He laughed and ran to grab the ring.

"Yes!" Daisy shouted, catching her ring.

June giggled as their ring fell at Ina's feet.

"Okay, partners, now you take the ring and send it back," Mrs. Kaufman instructed.

James returned. "Ready, Mrs. Weatherly?"

"I think so," she said without a hint of confidence in her voice.

He fired the ring into the air. It sailed high and she backed away, trying to aim her rods in the right direction. With a lunge, she snagged the ring and righted herself before she tumbled to the ground.

She paused to catch her breath and caught a snippet of conversation the two maids were having in hushed tones nearby.

"Did you see Gabe's face?" Tammy asked her friend. "The bruises and cuts look so painful."

"I know," the other maid replied. "A beautiful face like his getting all messed up like that is a real shame."

Maggie forgot all about the game and stared down the road, where she caught a glimpse of the blacksmith's shop. Her heart skipped a beat when she thought of one way Gabe might have recently sustained injury—if he had abducted Amanda, and she'd tried to fight him off.

Maggie would have to talk to the blacksmith sooner rather than later.

14

Gabe wore a tattered leather apron and drew red-hot metal out of a tall fireplace in the middle of the room, the chimney reaching to the rafters. He placed the glowing metal on an anvil and hammered it flat. A crowd stood around him as he described the process of forging steel. Maggie, who had made her excuses to James with great reluctance, listened and watched until the smithy demonstration ended and the group broke up.

She approached Gabe, and he stopped swinging the hammer, his arm in midair. His face was narrow, and he had big brown eyes and a neatly trimmed reddish-brown beard. His right eye was encircled by a deep purple bruise, and his lower lip was puffy and recently split open. Maggie thought of the scratches she had seen on Kyle's face and wondered whether Gabe would try to lie about the origins of his injuries too. Her knees grew weak at the thought of confronting a man she already believed to be violent, but she thought of the photo of Amanda, bound and undoubtedly frightened, and stiffened her resolve.

"You're that lady who's asking all the questions," he said before she could get out a word. "I figured you'd get to me eventually."

"Would you mind putting down your hammer as we talk?" she asked.

He stared at her for a long moment. "You don't really think I'd hurt you, do you? Right here in the middle of the village where everyone could see us? That'd be crazy."

Though he had a good point, people did crazy things all the time, and she preferred to play it safe.

He met her uncomfortable silence with a shrug, set the

hammer on a workbench, and put the tip of the iron into the fire. His apron flapped against his legs as he took big strides toward her. He cut an imposing figure, and it wasn't hard to imagine him getting into a brawl. She just hoped Amanda hadn't been involved in the altercation.

"Where did you get the bruises?" she asked.

He touched his face as if he'd forgotten about the injuries. "Kyle Jensen. We had a little fight on Thursday night."

Finally, a straight answer. "Was that after your shift had ended, down by the barn?"

"Yeah, about then."

"What did you fight about?"

"He'd heard a rumor that something was going on between me and Amanda."

"Was there?"

"Not really. I flirted with her and tried to start something up but didn't get very far."

"She wasn't interested?"

"C'mon, lady. You see this face?" He grinned and flexed his biceps. "And these guns? Why would she say no to that?"

"So she agreed to go out with you?"

"She sure did. She was supposed to meet me in the yard by the manor house on Thursday after work, but she didn't show up."

"But she had made plans to meet Lily then too."

He frowned. "Amanda was supposed to tell Lily that we were taking off. Guess she forgot."

Maggie appreciated his earnest responses, but she didn't much like the thought of this older man making advances to a high school girl. "Aren't you a little old for her?"

He lifted his shoulders into a hard line. "She's eighteen, and it isn't illegal. Besides, she wanted to go out with me. I wasn't forcing her."

Maggie remembered what Lily had said about the man Amanda might have been dating—that he was older, and possibly even married. Though Gabe didn't wear a wedding ring, she thought she'd find out as much as she could.

"Gabe, are you married by any chance?"

"Me? No way. I just can't be tied down." His smirk faded away, and his expression darkened. "Well, I was engaged last year. But she was completely crazy and left me. I mean, it was totally mutual, though." He shifted his feet uncomfortably.

He clearly doesn't handle rejection well. That's not a good sign.

"What did you do when Amanda didn't show up on Thursday?"

"I went into the manor to look for her. I found her mittens but no other sign of her, so I figured maybe she got confused and was waiting for me at my car. So I grabbed her mittens—"

"You took her mittens?"

"I thought she'd need them, but when Kyle got in my face, I dropped them and forgot all about them until I heard the police found them."

"Why didn't you tell the police about dropping them?"

"And tie me to her disappearance and some big investigation? No thanks."

"Why are you telling me now?"

"I heard Kyle's been talking to the cops, and I figured if I told someone about the mittens first, I'd be believed over any story Kyle would tell." He scowled. "If you ask me, Kyle's the one you should be talking to. He was about the only person around by that point, and what other reason would he have for hanging around at quitting time? He's been the first guy out the gate all week."

"Did you question Kyle about that?"

"Nah, I was just glad to get away from him. I still thought maybe Amanda got confused and was waiting for me at my car, but she wasn't there."

"So what did you do?"

"I called her. When she didn't answer, I got to thinking maybe Kyle had talked her out of meeting me, so I went back to the barn to see him."

Maggie couldn't imagine getting into a fistfight with someone and then returning to accost him, but she wasn't an aggressive young man who had something to prove.

"I found him in the haymow, changing into his street clothes," Gabe continued. "I thought he was changing to go home, but he said he got blood on his costume, and he didn't want to get into trouble."

"Your blood or Kyle's?"

"Don't know. He showed me the spot, and there was a lot of blood. I know neither one of us bled that much from a few scratches or a split lip."

Maggie had to wonder if during the time Gabe had gone to the car, Kyle had managed to hurt Amanda and hide her away somewhere. "Did you ask him about it?"

"He said it was from earlier in the day when an ox was cut on one of the barbed wire fences in the south pasture."

"And did you believe him?"

"Heck no I didn't believe him. I was worried that he'd found Amanda and taken his anger out on her, and now that she's missing, you gotta wonder if I was right."

Maggie was glad the detective had followed up and taken Kyle's clothes to test the blood for Amanda's DNA. "Did you ask him about Amanda's whereabouts?"

"He said that as far as he knew, she'd gone home with Lily."

"What did you do next?"

"I walked through the rest of the village, you know, to see if she was hurt somewhere. When I didn't find her, I thought she'd blown me off and left for the night."

"Where'd you go from here?"

He arched a brow and shook his head incredulously. "I tell you the truth, and you still think I had something to do with Amanda going missing."

"If you didn't, then you should be willing to tell me where you were so we can rule you out in Amanda's disappearance."

"Fine. I stopped at Peggy Sue's Diner in Weatherly for dinner and stayed there for an hour. Maybe more. Even though the waitresses wear roller skates, the service there is kind of slow."

"And last night? Where were you then?"

A low growl came from his throat. "Home. Alone. So yeah, I don't have an alibi for the break-in, but I bet Kyle doesn't either."

A pair of visitors came to the door, and Gabe's gaze darted to them. "Excuse me. I need to get back to work."

He went to greet them, and Maggie sought out a bench on the edge of town where she wouldn't be overheard and called Kyle's mother. Hannah wasn't happy to hear from Maggie, but she said Kyle didn't have access to a working printer at home. She also admitted before she hung up that Kyle hadn't been home last night as he'd claimed.

Why did Kyle think he could get away with using his mother as an alibi when she'd previously told Maggie the truth? Perhaps his plan was to keep buying time until he would release Amanda. But when would that be?

"Yoo-hoo! Maggie!" Ina hollered from the far side of the road. "Are you coming to the manor for lunch?"

As Ina crossed the road, Maggie glanced at her watch. She'd been so lost in her thoughts that she hadn't realized time had flown by. She was more eager than ever to talk to Kyle again, but her stomach was rumbling for Ingrid's delicious cooking, and she looked forward to spending quality time with her friends.

Ornery grin in place as always, Ina fell into step with Maggie, and she was taken aback by how perfect Ina looked in her traditional attire. She wore a blue bonnet that went well with her coloring, and her dress emphasized her trim figure.

Maggie took in the full velvet skirt, but when she glimpsed Ina's feet, she realized why the woman looked so at ease. "You're wearing your tennis shoes."

Ina lifted her skirt and wiggled a white canvas shoe. "I wasn't about to wear those torture devices a second day in a row."

Maggie grinned. "I wish I'd done the same."

"You can change at lunch."

"About that. I hadn't realized it was this late. I have something important to do first. I'll try to hurry and then join you all." Maggie stood. "I can walk with you since I'm heading for the barn."

"To speak to Kyle again." Ina put her hands on her hips. "He's a sly one, and I wouldn't be a bit surprised if he had something to do with Amanda's disappearance."

Maggie told her about the morning's developments. Ina's shrewd input was always invaluable to her. As they rounded the corner of the barn, she walked straight into Kyle.

"Speak of the devil." Ina crossed her arms, and her eyes narrowed.

"Glad I ran into you, Kyle," Maggie said. "I wanted to talk to you."

She expected a defensive reply, but he sighed and said, "Me too."

She stared at him. "You want to talk to me?"

"Yeah, my mom just called me. She said you were bugging her again. She nagged and nagged until I promised to tell the detective where I really was the last two nights."

"I think you're making the right choice, young man," Ina said sternly.

"As do I," Maggie added. "Let's start with where you were when Amanda disappeared."

"I was supposed to meet Gabe."

"You're friends with Gabe?" Maggie watched Kyle for any sign of deceit.

"Not really. We went to school together is all, but he ran with a rough crowd and I was a jock. He's been into illegal stuff for years. Petty things like breaking into houses. Boosted a car once too."

Maggie couldn't help but see the irony in the fact that Gabe—this alleged criminal—was the person who had seemed to be the most truthful with her so far.

Ina's eyes narrowed. "It's good that you steered clear of the likes of him, then."

"My mom says I should stay away from him now too. But he offered to help me out after I broke up with Amanda. I told him she dumped me because I didn't have any money and couldn't afford to buy her a big diamond. I figure if I can give her an amazing ring, she'll come back to me and marry me."

Despite her suspicions, her heart went out to the young man who clearly didn't want to accept the rejection of the girl he loved. "And Gabe offered to help you get the ring?"

"Sorta. He told me all about the scores he's made lately. Then he says it would be helpful to have a partner, and he'd split the money with me."

"Oh boy." Ina shook her head. "It's never a good idea to decide a life of crime is your destiny."

"What? Destiny?" His forehead furrowed. "It was nothing like that. I was gonna get together some extra dough to buy the ring, that's all."

"And then what?" Maggie asked. "If Amanda is only interested in money, wouldn't you need to keep stealing to provide the things you think she wants?"

He looked confused, as if this wasn't something he'd considered.

Ina jumped in, saving Kyle from answering. "So you've been

breaking into places with Gabe, and you were supposed to meet up with him on Thursday."

"Yeah. But then I found out that the jerk asked Amanda on a date and was going to meet me afterward. Can you believe it? Whatever happened to the bro code?"

"I'm pretty sure when you're 'bros' with a thief, you shouldn't expect him to have any kind of ethical code," Maggie said.

"Well, yeah. I guess I shoulda figured that out, right?"

That and so many other things at your age.

"Instead of going off with Gabe, you fought him," Ina said.

"I lost it, man. Really lost it. Told him to stay away from Amanda. He gets all Mr. Tough Guy, and I have to punch his lights out, you know?"

She didn't know, but she wanted to seem understanding all the same. "And that happened down by the barn?"

Kyle nodded.

Ina tsked. "Stealing and fighting. You're not heading in a good direction."

Maggie agreed. "Is that when you got blood on your costume?"

"Nah, that was from the stupid ox that walked right into a barbed wire fence on the south pasture. I had to bring him in so the vet could look at him."

"Why lie to me about that?" Maggie asked.

"I forgot to file a report, and I didn't want Radcliff to know. He'd probably fire me."

"And that night, then? What did you do if you didn't go out with Gabe?"

"Oh, I still did the job. But I'm not sharing the money with Gabe. No way. Not even if he gets mad."

"Why would you even tell him about it?"

"I need him to fence the stuff I boosted. He has those contacts, not me."

"So you don't really have an alibi."

"I have the things I took. And all you have to do is check the police records for the stuff taken in the break-in. It's all in my garage and it will prove I was there."

"I suppose you were the one who stole money from the apothecary too," Ina said.

He shrugged. "That was only a hundred bucks. This place can afford it."

She appreciated Kyle's newfound willingness to tell the truth. Maggie would still confirm the details of his break-in before eliminating him as a suspect, but one thing was certain. Gabe was now firmly planted on her list, and if his alibi didn't pan out, he'd shoot to the top with Craig and Ingrid.

15

Later that afternoon, Maggie stood in the parking lot and watched as Kyle was put into the back of Deputy Matthews's car with Detective Adams standing alongside.

"I can't believe Kyle confessed to those burglaries and he's being arrested," Ruth said. "It's sad to see a young person in that situation."

"I know. I feel bad for him, but he has to learn that there are consequences for his actions."

"Agreed. On the bright side, if he doesn't have a record, he might only get probation, and this might be the wake-up call he needs."

Maggie unlocked Jasmine's van and gathered up her skirt so she could sidle into the driver's seat. "I hope I can drive in this dress. I thought about changing, but I can't wait to see the look on people's faces when we walk into that diner dressed like this." Maggie adjusted the seat and mirrors and was soon steering down the country road toward town. "I'm glad the snow has melted a bit."

"I am so looking forward to spring." Ruth sighed. "This late snow and cold snap is starting to wear on me."

"It sure is pretty on the open fields, though."

Ruth turned her head to look out the windows, and they moved on to a conversation about the spring fund-raiser for the historical society. Before Maggie knew it, she was parking outside the low-slung diner, its arched entry ringed with glowing neon lights to give the façade the appearance of a gigantic jukebox.

"This ought to be fun," Ruth said as she slid out of the passenger-side door.

They passed under the neon lights and stepped onto a black-and-white checkered floor. Pink vinyl chairs surrounded chrome-and-laminate tables, and pink-capped stools were lined up in front of a Formica-and-chrome bar.

"Something about this reminds me of The Busy Bean," Ruth whispered.

"I was thinking the same thing," Maggie said as she noticed a woman behind the bar dressed in a black poodle skirt with a white-and-pink checked blouse and a pink leather belt. Her blonde hair was piled high on her head and pink lipstick was generously slathered on her lips. "I could easily see Daisy in that outfit."

Wondering if she might be the manager, Maggie glanced around the room to find diners staring at them. She'd expected to be gawked at, but she didn't think she would feel this conspicuous.

"You got the wrong era," a guy called out.

Maggie self-consciously wrestled her skirt into submission to take a seat at the counter.

"Ladies." The woman behind the bar, whose blouse was embroidered with the name *Peggy*, smiled at them as she handed each of them a laminated menu. "What can I get you?"

Maggie assumed Peggy was the owner and would be a good person to ask about Gabe, but the large picture of a chocolate shake on the menu in front of her was too hard to resist.

Maggie looked at Ruth. "I know it's cold outside, but do you want to order a chocolate shake?"

"I make a pretty mean shake," Peggy added.

"No need to twist my arm," Ruth replied.

"Coming right up."

"This feels so weird," Ruth said, looking around at the diners staring at them. "It's like we're a couple of antiques on display at your shop."

"You come up with the most interesting ways to look at things," Maggie said. "You're definitely an outside-the-box thinker."

The milk shake machine whirred into action, interrupting their talk, so they sat watching Peggy lift the tin mixing cup up and down on the blender arm. She poured thick creamy chocolate into two vintage glasses and set them on the counter. Maggie quickly opened a straw and took a long drink.

"You're right. You do make a mean shake."

Peggy grinned, then leaned her elbows on the counter as if ready to settle in for a long conversation. "I assume you ladies are participating at the Weatherly Village thing this weekend."

"Mm-hm," Maggie hummed, her mouth too full of the frozen, chocolaty goodness for her to speak.

"So what brings you to my diner?"

Maggie released the straw and swallowed a mouthful of milk shake. "Could we talk to you about Gabe Hendricks?"

"That guy." Peggy's lip curled. "What'd he do now?"

"Nothing other than tell me he had dinner here on Thursday night, and I wanted to confirm that."

"Are you kidding me?" Peggy's voice rose an octave. "Not only was he not here Thursday night, but even if he *had* shown up, I'd have kicked him out. He's trouble with a capital *T*. He's rowdy and gets into fights at the drop of a hat. And he's been arrested for all kinds of things."

"What about the other waitresses? Might they have seen him?"

"I was the only one working that night. I like to give the girls time off when I can, and we were pretty slow."

Maggie was disheartened to learn that Gabe had been lying to her about being here, but she also found it odd that he'd chosen this place as an alibi when he must have known Maggie could easily find out the truth.

"Has he been in trouble recently?" Maggie asked. Though

Kyle had already told her about Gabe's illegal activities, she wanted additional details.

Peggy scrunched up her penciled-in eyebrows. "What's this all about?"

Maggie explained.

"I heard about Amanda. Sweet kid. I hope you find her." Peggy frowned again. "Wouldn't put it past Gabe to be involved somehow."

"You mentioned he got into trouble," Ruth said. "What kinds of things did he do?"

"Nothing really. At least not since high school. Back then it was small-time break-ins."

"But nothing lately," Ruth clarified.

"No. I don't think he's stopped, though. He's just gotten better at it, so he's not getting caught."

"Do you think Gabe could hurt or abduct a girl?" Maggie asked.

"You mean Amanda." Peggy drummed her fingers on the counter. "Yeah, sure. With his temper and him thinking every woman should swoon as his feet, if Amanda snubbed him, I could see him taking it pretty hard."

Maggie shared a knowing look with Ruth as the front door bells tinkled. An older couple made their way to the counter and sat, their gazes fixed on Maggie and Ruth in their anachronistic garb.

"If that's all," Peggy said, straightening up, "I've got to get back to my customers."

"I'll just need the check when you get a chance." Maggie turned her attention back to the shake.

"So he lied to you," Ruth said. "And he didn't give a very good alibi, considering it took you no time at all to poke holes in it."

"So why do it? He knew I was asking questions, and he had to know Detective Adams was too, which means he should have had ample time to think of something better."

Ruth twirled her straw in her glass. "Could he *want* you to find out what he's up to?"

"Maybe he was just trying to waste my time. At least the two of us got to spend some time together and have a little treat."

Ruth slurped the last of her shake. "That we did, my friend."

Maggie paid the bill, and they drove back to the village. Throughout the afternoon she talked to other workers, but she learned nothing new. During dinner, she provided a brief update on Amanda. Afterward, in the library, Mr. Radcliff gave them an overview of the evening's activities. As hosts, James and Maggie needed to provide refreshments, but fortunately Ingrid had prepared the treats, and they only had to retrieve and serve them later on.

Together they all set up tables with cribbage, checkers, dominoes, and pickup sticks.

"While June may be a champion checkers player," Daisy said, "I am the master at pickup sticks, so I'd steer clear of both of us tonight."

"Hear, hear," June said as she placed checkers on the board.

James opened a mahogany-cased chess set with an inlaid interior board and turned-wood pieces. "Consider it a favor to everyone here that I won't be playing, or else you'd also have to avoid the chess table."

Laughter spilled through the room, and workers soon joined them. James took charge and encouraged everyone to settle in and choose a game they enjoyed. Maggie circulated among the tables, and wherever she encountered a lull, she tossed out conversation starters to encourage friendly chatter. When everyone was laughing and offering fun-loving taunts, she stepped back with James to watch.

"Well, Mrs. Weatherly," he said. "Our first hosting event as husband and wife seems to be a roaring success."

"I couldn't agree more, Mr. Weatherly." She smiled at him. "But I suppose we shouldn't get ahead of ourselves. We still need to handle the refreshments."

He made a sweeping gesture with his hand. "Then let us away to the kitchen with all haste."

She giggled and made her way to the kitchen, where they found Mr. Radcliff wearing his hat and coat and pulling open the outside door.

"Are you leaving for the night?" Maggie asked.

"I am. Fortunately Oliver fixed the door so I can lock up nice and tight."

A buzzing noise coming from across the room caught Maggie's attention. "What's that sound?"

"Oh, that." Mr. Radcliff shined his light on a wooden box and then lifted the lid. "Our beeswax candle vendor had plans tonight, and she couldn't let her demonstration hive sit in her cold car. So she asked me to keep the hive here overnight. I had it in my office, but it's not heated at night so I'm leaving them here where it's warm."

Maggie moved closer and looked at the bees. "I thought bees slept at night."

"I know nothing about them," Mr. Radcliff said. "You'll have to get information on their sleeping habits from their owner."

James frowned at the hive. "I once had a nest of wasps in my bedroom wall, and they buzzed all night long. It was like this sound only ten times louder. It almost felt like the wall was vibrating."

"How did you figure out what it was?" Maggie asked.

"I discovered on the Internet that the sound was the wasps fanning their hive to keep it cool. When I read that they sometimes ate the drywall and could come right through the wall, I got on the phone to a pest control expert."

Maggie shuddered at the thought. "I'm okay with honeybees, but that's disturbing."

"Tell me about it." James crossed to the big island, where plates of cookies and large pitchers waited.

"Best of luck with the remainder of the evening." Mr. Radcliff tipped his hat at them and stepped out the door.

Maggie moved to the island. "We'll have to make several trips."

James picked up a platter and a pitcher. "If only the butler and maids weren't playing games and could help us."

Maggie wrinkled her nose. "You're playing the role of gentleman unused to any labor quite perfectly."

"You, my good wife, could take lessons from me." He chuckled.

They placed the refreshments on a folding table set up in the dining room and then made several additional trips before announcing the food was served.

By the time the night was over and the last guest had departed, Maggie was exhausted, and her feet hurt something fierce. "I can't wait to get these shoes off."

She received a murmur of agreement from her friends as they climbed the stairs together. Maggie shed her gown and hung it up, then settled into the downy bed and fell fast asleep.

The next thing she knew, she was startled awake by a high, shrill scream. Surprised to see the gray light of dawn streaming through her window, she glanced at the clock. Six o'clock. She jumped from bed and dressed as quickly as she could. Out in the hallway, she found James emerging from his room and rubbing his eyes.

"You heard it too?" he asked.

"It was hard to miss. I think it came from downstairs, and I'm going to check it out."

"I'll come with you."

"We have to be quiet," she whispered as they crept down the stairs.

They eased through the drawing room, their footfalls silent. Then into the library. Next through the sitting room.

"Help! Someone help!"

"That came from the kitchen." She charged into the hallway and burst into the kitchen, James right behind her, to find the young maid Tammy standing over Ingrid's prone figure.

Tammy met Maggie's gaze. "I think she's dead. I came to work and found her like this."

James squatted and checked her pulse. He looked up to meet Maggie's eyes and shook his head.

Maggie put her arm around Tammy's quivering shoulders and guided her to a chair in the corner where she could no longer see Ingrid. Maggie located a glass on a nearby shelf and poured water for Tammy.

As Tammy calmed, Maggie took a better look at Ingrid. Two red welts stood out on the cook's face and another marred her neck. An EpiPen rested on her open palm. Several dead bees lay on the floor next to Ingrid's body. Her purse rested a few feet away, the contents scattered on the floor. The observation hive lay next to the door, a large crack in the side and several bees buzzing around it.

"Is Ingrid allergic to bees?" Maggie asked Tammy.

Tammy shrugged. "I don't know anything about her."

"I'm going to run outside to get a signal and call 911 and Detective Adams," she told James. Before he could respond, she raced down the hallway and out the door. She didn't stop running until she had two bars. Maggie called 911 and made sure to tell the operator that the gate was closed, so the EMTs would have to find another way to the manor house.

Next, she dialed Detective Adams.

"Hello," he answered after the fourth ring.

"I'm sorry to disturb you," she said. "We just found Ingrid, the cook at the manor house. She's on the kitchen floor. She's not breathing and has no pulse. The beekeeper left a demonstration hive in the kitchen, and I think Ingrid might have been stung. She has what looks like an EpiPen in her hand, so she might have been allergic to bees."

"Call 911 to get an ambulance out there."

"I did, but after the conversation I heard between her and her stepson, I don't think this was an accident."

"I'll be there in twenty minutes. Make sure you don't touch anything, and keep everyone except emergency responders out of the room."

"Will do." Maggie hung up and made her way back to the house where she found James, June, Ina, and Ruth huddled in conversation under the arched doorway to the sitting room. They used hushed tones, probably so Tammy wouldn't hear them from where she sat on the sofa.

Maggie joined her friends. "An ambulance and Detective Adams are on the way."

James gestured at Tammy. "I thought it would be best for her to get out of the kitchen."

"Good plan," Maggie said.

"James told us about Ingrid," June said. "Do you think she was allergic to bees?"

"I'm sure of it. What's unclear to me is whether or not the hive was broken on purpose."

June shuddered. "I hate to think there was a murderer in the house with us last night."

"Me too," Ruth said.

Maggie agreed, but she pushed the thought aside. "Would one of you sit with Tammy while I wait for the EMTs on the porch and direct them to the kitchen?"

"I'm glad to do it," Ruth offered.

"Me too," June added.

"I'll go to the kitchen in case someone should try to enter through that door," James said.

As everyone took their positions, Maggie thought about the day ahead. About her friends who had looked forward to this weekend for weeks, and should be dressed in their period attire and soon sitting down to breakfast in the historic house without a care in the world. Instead, this had proved to be a very difficult time. Aunt Evelyn had said that a full tummy was often the best cure after a terrible ordeal, and the sentiment had gotten young Maggie through the nights she'd spent at Sedgwick Manor, wide awake after a bad dream or a bump in the night. The recollection gave her an idea.

"June," Maggie called after her friend. "Maybe you could run down to the parking lot and tell Daisy what's happened. There will be no food served this morning, so we should get something from town, and Daisy's the best person to organize that."

"I don't know how you can think of food at a time like this." June wrung her hands.

"We'll all feel a little better after having some breakfast, especially Tammy. She probably won't be able to eat, but she could use some tea or coffee, and we won't be allowed in the kitchen."

"I'll be glad to take care of it," June said. "Let me get my coat, and I'm on my way."

"Thank you." Maggie jogged up the stairs to retrieve her coat and boots, then went out to wait on the porch.

Sirens sounded in the distance, and Maggie stomped her feet to keep warm until a pair of EMTs trudged up the road. She waved at them, and their steps quickened. She warned them about the bees in case they were allergic as she showed them to the kitchen. The EMTs quickly ascertained that there was nothing they could do for Ingrid.

Detective Adams and the deputy arrived shortly thereafter. He conferred with the EMTs and sent them on their way, then instructed the deputy to return to his car and call the medical examiner.

When Detective Adams crossed the room, Maggie said, "You should know that James and I walked over to Ingrid to check for a pulse, and then I helped Tammy sit in the chair in the corner and got her a glass of water. We didn't touch anything else."

He snapped on latex gloves as he looked over the room. "We haven't yet determined that this is a crime scene, ma'am. At first glance, I would say this appears to be a tragic accident. Maybe the deceased was carrying the hive outside and dropped it herself."

"If she was allergic to bees, I find it hard to believe she would touch the box."

"We haven't confirmed the allergy component."

"But she has an EpiPen in her hand."

He picked up the pen and studied it before shaking out an evidence bag and placing the device inside. "You're right. It's an EpiPen. But she might have been having a reaction to something else. We'll need to have her examined to know for sure."

Maggie knew he didn't distrust her judgment, but he had to check every single detail, especially if it turned out they were dealing with murder. She couldn't imagine the tremendous pressure he was under.

"Can we call her stepson, Craig Baldwin?" Maggie asked. "As I mentioned before, he works at the inn, but he isn't scheduled to arrive for some time. I think he lives with Ingrid, and his number should be in her cell phone, if she has one."

He shot her a look, his eyes kind but his tone solemn. "I *do* know how to do my job, Ms. Watson."

"I'm sorry, Officer. I wasn't trying to imply that you didn't. I was just trying to be helpful."

"If you want to be helpful, how about finding the beekeeper to do something about the bees so no one else gets stung?"

"We'll have to call Mr. Radcliff for that. I don't have his phone number, and even if I did, I can't get a signal in the house."

The detective pulled a radio from his pocket and ordered the deputy on patrol nearby to find Mr. Radcliff and escort him to the manor house. He then took his time looking at everything in the room. Maggie watched, feeling a little uncomfortable and wishing he'd say something or dismiss her. After a thorough search, he stooped to pick up Ingrid's cell phone.

"Her phone has a signal, albeit a weak one." He tapped a few buttons, then held it to his ear. "This is Detective Adams. We spoke the other day. I'm sorry to tell you that your stepmother has had an accident."

He explained about the beehive, and Maggie was surprised that he kept referring to it as an accident. She supposed it could be his way of making the incident seem less terrible for the victim's family, but she also knew that Detective Adams was right when he said that they couldn't rule out an accident at this point. Maggie listened carefully and could hear Craig's raised voice, but she couldn't make out his words.

"We thought she might be allergic," Detective Adams said into the phone.

"I'm still not convinced this was an accident," James said quietly from beside her.

"Neither am I," she told him. "You don't have to hang around here. June is arranging for breakfast and coffee to be brought in, and I know how much you like your morning coffee."

"How about I get ready for the day, and if you're not in the dining room when the coffee arrives, I'll bring a cup to you?"

"You really are the sweetest man, James Bennett." She rested a hand on his arm and let her gaze linger. Her heart warmed at the care she saw reflected back at her.

"Baldwin will be here soon," the detective said, interrupting the moment and bringing them sharply back to the situation at hand.

Maggie gave James's arm a quick squeeze, and he departed.

"You don't need to stay, Ms. Watson," Detective Adams said.

"If this is related to Ingrid and Craig's conversation that I overheard, it might help if I was here when he gives his statement."

"I'll allow it if you promise not to speak unless spoken to."

She mimicked zipping her mouth.

"I don't want to question him here in the kitchen. Could you suggest a private location for that?"

"The library would be perfect."

"Then go ahead and wait for us there." He turned away to wait for Craig.

Maggie stepped into the hallway, where she found a harried-looking Mr. Radcliff.

"I spoke to Tammy on the way in, and she gave me the details," he said. "This is terrible news. Just terrible."

"I wholeheartedly agree," Maggie said. "Did you know Ingrid was allergic to bees?"

He crossed his arms. "Do you think that if I'd known she was allergic, I'd have put the beehive in the kitchen?"

"How long has she worked here?"

"Ten or so years."

"And she never mentioned it? Not once in ten years, and it isn't on her employment papers?"

"Ingrid kept to herself, and we have nothing on our forms for allergies." He held out a folder labeled with Ingrid's name. "But you can be sure I'm going to start asking employees from now on."

"Detective Adams is in the kitchen." She moved aside to let him pass. "I imagine since you put the hive in there, he'll want to talk to you."

His chin rose. "You make it sound like I put it there to harm her."

"I'm just stating facts, Mr. Radcliff."

"Yes, but . . ." he spluttered and trailed off, gaping at her instead.

Maggie looked beyond his shock for other emotions and thought she saw guilt.

Could he be denying knowledge of the allergy because he had killed Ingrid? Maybe he'd kidnapped Amanda and Ingrid had confronted him. With the mounting evidence against the other people in the town, Maggie hadn't considered him a viable suspect.

Until now.

16

In the library with the doors closed, Maggie held a cup of fresh coffee in her hands and sat in a chair in the corner as directed by Detective Adams.

"I can't believe she's dead." Face pale, Craig grasped the edges of a wide mahogany desk.

Detective Adams took a step closer to Craig. "Were the two of you close?"

"Not really. She only married my dad a couple of years ago, and then Dad was killed in a car crash a few months after that. He left the house to her, and she's let me stay on."

He didn't sound the least bit broken up about Ingrid's death. *But shock could be clouding his emotions*, Maggie thought.

"Did you hear her leave home last night?" Detective Adams asked.

"No, and I was home all night. Who would have put bees in the kitchen anyway?"

The detective explained Mr. Radcliff's reasons for leaving the bees in a warm place.

"Then he should have told her that was what he was going to do. She'd never have come in here if she'd known about the bees."

The detective's eyebrow arched. "Did Mr. Radcliff know about her allergy?"

"Doubtful. She always said she thought it made her seem weak. Besides, she didn't share much about her personal life at work. Or ever, really. Shoot, I live with her and don't know hardly anything about her past. But still, Radcliff should have asked first."

Detective Adams didn't respond but kept his gaze on Craig.

"Do you think someone put the hive in the kitchen and intentionally broke it open?" Craig ran a hand through his hair. "You know, to kill Ingrid on purpose?"

"Can you think of a reason why someone would want to kill her?"

Craig looked away and shrugged.

The detective widened his stance. "Ms. Watson overheard a conversation in the kitchen stairwell in which Ingrid mentioned that you were an illegitimate heir to the Weatherly estate."

Craig spun and eyed Maggie, his eyes wide with shock. "You followed me that night and then told the cops?"

"You were acting suspicious at the inn," she replied. "Then you disappeared into a secret stairwell. I had no choice."

"Unbelievable." Craig glared at Maggie, and if looks could kill, his would have done her in.

"Could Ingrid's death be related to the inheritance you mentioned in that conversation?" the detective asked.

"*Alleged* conversation."

Maggie wanted to comment on his response, but she had promised to keep quiet unless spoken to, so she clamped her mouth shut.

"Your need to point out that it was alleged tells me that you're probably hiding something. As does your avoidance of the question." Detective Adams fixed his gaze on Craig.

He didn't squirm, and Maggie was impressed. She would have wilted under the detective's intense scrutiny whether she was guilty or not.

"If you are involved in anything illegal," Detective Adams continued, "it will come out in the investigation into your step-mother's death, and it would go better for you if you admitted it now."

Craig bit the inside of his cheek, glanced down at his feet, and sighed. "Fine. We've been taking money from the inn for quite some time, but it's rightfully my money anyway."

"But—" Maggie began, but stopped at Detective Adams's sharp look in her direction.

"How do you figure it's your money?" the detective asked Craig.

"After my dad died, Ingrid got interested in family history. I think it was her way of keeping him close to her. She discovered that I'm a Weatherly, but not by name. My ancestor had a child out of wedlock, and I'm descended from that line. Now I'm the only living Weatherly heir, and we tried to get the estate to recognize my rights, but they laughed in my face."

"So you're taking the inheritance you deserve." The detective sounded like he sympathized and agreed with Craig, but Maggie could see it was a ploy to keep the younger man talking.

"Yeah, wouldn't you?"

"Do you think someone discovered your theft and confronted your stepmother?"

Maggie applauded Detective Adams's ability to sidestep Craig's question.

The younger man shrugged.

Amanda. Now's the time to ask about Amanda.

"Someone like Amanda Caldwell?"

Perfect. Maggie couldn't have timed it any better herself.

"Amanda?" Craig frowned. "We had nothing to do with Amanda."

Maggie couldn't stay silent any longer. "Then why did you tell Ingrid that you were worried about me asking around?"

He didn't even acknowledge her and remained mute, staring at the floor.

"You might want to rethink that non-answer, Mr. Baldwin," Detective Adams said. "Unless you cooperate, I can arrest you for obstructing an investigation."

Craig crossed his arms. "It's simple. I figured if Ms. Watson kept digging, she'd find out about the money, and I'm not going to jail for taking what's rightfully mine."

"Perhaps as I continued to ask more questions, Ingrid got worried and was going to tell the police what she knows. You didn't want her to report you, so—"

"You think *I* killed her? You're nuts."

"You seem to be one of the few people who knew about her allergy," Detective Adams said mildly.

"Okay, back up. When we first started talking you said it was an accident, now all of a sudden you think she's been murdered. Which one is it?"

"It's too early in the investigation to tell," Detective Adams replied.

"You said you were home last night, and if Ingrid was here, that means you were home alone," Maggie stated, and the detective joined Craig in glaring at her for her continued interference. She felt her cheeks grow pink, but she pressed on, certain she could get to the bottom of this mystery if only Craig would tell the whole story.

Craig narrowed his eyes. "That's what I said."

"Then you don't have an alibi," she pointed out, noticing Detective Adams had opened his mouth as if to speak over her.

"I can't help it if I was alone."

"No you can't," the detective added, and Maggie feared he was about to rule Craig out as a suspect.

"But—"

"But unless we can prove your whereabouts," Detective Adams interrupted, "you will remain a person of interest."

"Yes," Maggie agreed, and Detective Adams heaved a frustrated sigh. Maggie pretended to zip her lips again to mollify him, but with murder potentially added to the kidnapper's charges, she'd keep Craig as a suspect too.

"Now that you've confessed to embezzlement, I'll have to notify Mr. Radcliff, and if he wants to press charges, you'll be arrested."

Craig scowled. "But my stepmother just died."

"Perhaps Mr. Radcliff will take that into account, but right now, I want you to accompany me to his office to discuss the theft." The detective looked at Maggie. "Thank you for your help, Ms. Watson. I'll take it from here. Please let me know if you find out anything else." Detective Adams marched Craig from the room, leaving Maggie alone.

The doors on the nineteenth-century Black Forest cuckoo clock in the corner opened, and a painted bird and seated Bavarian gentleman slid out. Maggie allowed her mind to wander as she admired the detailed carving of a stag's head and the oak leaf branches laden with acorns that lined the sides.

She was jolted from her reverie when the clock fell silent again; it was later than she'd realized, and she needed to get ready for the church service. She was looking forward to it. Church always soothed her soul. She returned to her room to put on her gown and the dreaded shoes. A spot on her foot stung where it had been rubbed raw the day before as she hurried down the stairs to join the group.

On the way to the small chapel, her friends fired off questions about Ingrid's death and the detective's investigation of Craig, and Maggie answered them as best she could until she caught sight of the charming chapel. Jasmine, Lily, and Daisy stood waiting on the narrow pathway leading up to the chapel doors.

"Why don't we hold off talking about Ingrid around Lily," she suggested.

"Yes, let's try to shield her from any additional stress. She's dealing with quite enough for a young girl," Ina replied, and the group murmured their agreement.

Maggie put a smile on her face and greeted the trio.

"Did everyone get enough to eat this morning?" Daisy asked.

"It was perfect. Thank you again for making sure we had a meal," Ruth said.

"I'm glad I could help. I've already spoken to the manager of the local diner, and she'll help arrange today's lunch too."

The church bells pealed above, signaling that the service was about to begin. With a start, Maggie realized that their weekend would be over after lunch and everyone would be returning to Somerset Harbor. She couldn't leave the village with Amanda still missing. Not when she'd promised Lily she'd do everything she could to find her friend.

Maggie approached Daisy. "Can we talk for a minute?"

"Sure thing, doll. Is everything okay?"

Maggie slowed until they fell behind the group. "I was wondering if you'd thought about what you're going to do if Amanda isn't located by the time the village closes today."

"I've already committed to Jasmine and Lily that I'm staying here until she's found."

"Can you keep your motor home on the property?"

"I asked Mr. Radcliff, and he's checking with the board of directors. Jasmine offered to let me park at her house, but if Mr. Radcliff says I can't stay here, I'll park on the side of the road. I won't be far from the location where Amanda was last seen."

"But you wouldn't have electricity or water."

"I have the battery for heat, and I'll manage the rest."

Maggie couldn't imagine living without the necessities, but she wasn't going to let a little discomfort sway her from helping in the search for Amanda. "If June can cover the shop, can I stay with you?"

"I'd be delighted. I'm so thankful you want to stay. You are the best kind of friend." Daisy linked her arm with Maggie's, and they entered the small chapel.

Maggie took a moment to look around the simple interior with its white plaster walls and vaulted ceiling. A simple wood podium sat in front, and five box pews lined each side, reminding her with a pang of homesickness of Old Faith Chapel back home. Wearing a basic black cassock with buttons running down the front and a white cravat at the neck, the minister stood in front. A roadmap of wrinkles was etched into his kind face.

With no room left in the pew beside their friends, Maggie and Daisy sat behind them. Maggie glanced around and noted several village workers in attendance, but not Mr. Radcliff or any of Maggie's suspects except Gabe. She had to admit surprise at seeing him there.

When the service started, her mind kept wandering to Amanda's disappearance, but she continued to drag it back to the service until the end, when the minister offered a prayer for Amanda's safe return and for Ingrid's family. Maggie added her earnest plea too.

At the door, she went to shake hands with the minister, but Gabe intercepted her.

"I want to come clean," he said.

"Come clean?" she asked.

"Yeah. It's rough what happened to Ingrid, and I don't want that to happen to Amanda, so I don't want you wasting any time on looking into me."

"Okay," Maggie said, eyeing him warily.

"I lied about going to the diner."

"And if you didn't do anything wrong, why would you lie?"

"I went out with this other chick in town and didn't want Amanda to find out about it." He clamped a hand on the back of his neck. "I liked Amanda — really liked her — and I was kinda thinking we could still go out. You know, when she was found."

Maggie asked for the girl's contact information, but she had learned to be skeptical of Gabe's alibis, and she didn't think this girl he had supposedly been out with could be trusted. Oddly enough, though, she was starting to trust Gabe.

"I'm not lying," he stated emphatically, as if he could hear her thoughts. "I'm right here where God could strike me dead, so I'm not about to lie."

Maggie swallowed her amusement at this interesting piece of doctrine. "Thanks for letting me know." She excused herself and hurried to join her friends on the path. "The minister had already heard about Ingrid," she said to the group, "and I thought news traveled fast in Somerset Harbor."

"I told him before the service," Jasmine said. "He mentioned praying for Amanda, and I told him about Ingrid so he could add her family to his prayers too."

Maggie opened her mouth to thank Jasmine for her kindness, but she saw Detective Adams heading for the gate. "You'll have to excuse me. I need to talk to the detective."

She jogged down the street, which was nearly impossible in the long dress and pinching shoes that nearly brought tears to her eyes, but she had to catch him before he left.

"Detective Adams," she called out when she could run no more.

He turned, and even from a distance, she saw his chest rise and fall in an exasperated sigh. She chided herself for being so brash when he'd questioned Craig that morning, but she wouldn't let a bit of irritation put her off.

"Are you finished with the crime scene?" she asked, gasping for breath.

"I am."

"And do you think a crime has been committed?"

"Are you asking if I think Ingrid was murdered?"

She nodded, grasping at a stitch in her side.

"I honestly don't know at this point in the investigation."

"Are you leaning that way at least?"

"Ms. Watson, it almost sounds like you're hoping that she was murdered."

"I would never hope that someone was murdered. I just want to know if it's a fact. A lot of strange things have been happening around here this weekend, and I'm wondering if it's all related somehow."

"I'm afraid I can't help you with that. As I said, I don't know if this was an accident or not." He ran a hand over already rumpled hair. "And unless a witness or the killer, if there is one, suddenly comes forward, we may never know if the hive was broken accidentally or on purpose."

"Maybe if we figured out when she died, that could help narrow down our suspects. Do you know her time of death?"

"The medical examiner arrived shortly after I interviewed Baldwin. At that time, she said Ingrid had been dead less than twelve hours."

Maggie ticked off the hours in her head to determine that Ingrid had died around ten p.m.

"Now if you'll excuse me," the detective said, "I need to follow up on a few leads."

"Is the kitchen still off-limits?" Maggie asked.

"Not that you'll find anything there that my team missed, but you're welcome to have another look. The beekeeper has retrieved her hive, but there are still a few bees around, so be careful."

Determined to prove him wrong, and to change her shoes, Maggie turned, then remembered Craig.

"Before you go, Detective," she called out, "what happened with Craig Baldwin?"

"Radcliff is reviewing his records, and if he finds evidence of embezzlement, he'll press charges. Until that time, Baldwin will remain free."

"But he could flee the area."

"He's been warned against doing anything of the sort, but when it comes to embezzlement charges, there is no crime without a victim. Mr. Radcliff will have to prove the theft and decide to press charges before I can arrest anyone."

Maggie didn't like the thought of Craig getting away with theft, but the detective had to follow the law.

"I understand," she said and turned to catch up with her friends. They'd disappeared in the milling crowd so she hurried ahead, limping a little with her sore foot. Near the manor, she spotted June at an antique dealer's booth and waved.

"You look like you're in a hurry," June said, falling into step beside her.

"I am. The detective is finished with the kitchen, and I want to have another look around before anything is disturbed."

"Mind if I tag along?"

"Are you kidding? I'd love it. Two heads are better than one, as they say."

"And as I always reply, that depends on the two heads."

Maggie chuckled. "I had a chance to visit the dealers with James yesterday and spotted some amazing items that I reserved for the shop. Did you find anything you liked?"

"Oh yes, and the vendor I was just talking to gave me information about an upcoming estate sale that sounds very promising. I think we could pick up some great things for the shop, and we should plan to attend."

"Sounds great—" Maggie stopped short as she saw Kyle crossing the road ahead.

"But?" June prompted.

"But what?"

"It sounded liked you were going to add something."

"No . . . no. The sale sounds very promising. My mind just keeps going back to Amanda. Sorry."

"No need to apologize. I wish I could help too."

They climbed the stairs to the manor and entered.

"I don't know about you," Maggie said, "but I have to get out of these shoes."

"I was hoping someone would suggest that so I wouldn't be the only one out of costume."

"Don't worry." Maggie grinned and started up the stairs. "Ina is wearing her tennies too."

June stopped on the upstairs landing and adjusted her dress. "I'll be ever so grateful to put this outfit away for good."

"I'll meet you back out here in a few minutes." Maggie half expected to find another note on her pillow, but the pillows were bare. She lifted them up to be sure and when she found nothing, she was overwhelmed by a mixture of relief and disappointment. After Ingrid's death, Maggie would have liked further confirmation that Amanda was alive, but she was glad to know that no intruders had crept into her room when she wasn't there.

Maggie undid the laces of the black leather shoes and rubbed her sore feet before putting on her sneakers. She thought about changing out of the dress too, but she wanted to honor the spirit of the weekend, so she left the room and met June in the hallway.

June stuck out her foot. "Better?"

Maggie let out an exaggerated sigh. "Much better."

At the kitchen doorway, Maggie paused to survey the space. She thought back to her first day in the kitchen and tried to find any item that seemed out of place.

"I know we're supposed to be looking for clues," June said as she crossed the room, "but this pie safe is calling out to me. It's an amazing example of primitive techniques."

Maggie joined June and studied the pattern of punched stars and hearts on the turquoise-colored pie safe. "Seeing it in this kitchen and being dressed like this makes it so easy to imagine using the pie safe in everyday life."

"I may not like the clothing we've had to wear, but it really has brought history to life for me. Our pieces in the shop have taken on a whole new dimension. This pie safe has seen so much."

"I wonder what color it's painted inside." Maggie reached out to run a hand over the tin panels, then remembered the signs posted all around the house telling them not to touch the antiques.

"We could look," June suggested.

"But we're not supposed to."

"The signs, you mean? Those are for the general public, but antique experts like us . . ." June trailed off and winked conspiratorially.

Maggie didn't need further encouragement. She took hold of the single knob and pulled it open. She took in every detail of the interior, which turned out to be painted to match the outside.

"That's odd." She leaned closer to one of the hinges. "The screws are machined."

June moved closer. "An authentic piece from this time would have handmade hardware. Maybe it's been repaired."

"If so, they could have at least located the right kind of screws." She studied the actual hinges. "All of the hinges are machined too."

"A reproduction?" June met Maggie's gaze.

"But how could that be? The brochure states that only a few of the items on the property are reproductions. Everything else is original."

"Maybe the brochure is wrong."

"But Mr. Radcliff confirmed it. He's very knowledgeable about antiques. At least about the ones at the village. He couldn't have made such an obvious mistake. I need to talk to him again, and this time, I'll press for more details." She closed the safe and met June's gaze. "It's starting to look like Mr. Radcliff is hiding something, just like everyone else in this village."

17

Maggie wanted to go straight to Mr. Radcliff, but June convinced her that it would be better if they researched the value of the pie safe first, to see if it was worth enough that hiding the reproduction might be a motive for abducting Amanda or killing Ingrid. On the way to the motor home to use a computer, they ran into James, who joined them.

Maggie sat across the small dining table from James, and June sat next to Maggie. On Lily's break, she'd taught them how to use June's smartphone to create something Lily had called a "hot spot," which would allow them to connect to the Internet on her laptop, and fortunately they were able to get a strong-enough signal.

Maggie'd had no idea a phone could be used in this way, and even after watching Lily make the connections, Maggie doubted she could do it herself in the future. She'd always counted on her daughter to help her out with technology, but with Emily out of the house now, Maggie needed to learn to keep up. For now, she'd be fine using a notepad and pen as she reviewed the leads while June searched the Internet.

Maggie tapped her pen on the pad. "Okay, so what do we know for sure?"

"The pie safe is a fake," June replied.

Maggie noted it on her pad. "But why? Was it always a reproduction, and this is proof the estate was swindled a long time ago, or has someone replaced the original with the reproduction more recently?"

"For insurance purposes, I would imagine that Mr. Radcliff

would have had some sort of documentation proving it was an original piece when he took over as manager," James said.

"Like an appraisal, you mean?" June asked.

"Right. From a reputable dealer, of course."

"When I meet with Mr. Radcliff, I'll ask him to show me any documentation he has on this piece." Maggie flipped the page on her pad and wrote *Questions for Mr. Radcliff* on the top of the page. She made a bullet point and wrote *Appraisal documents?*

"Since he told you the antiques are all original, let's assume they once were," James said. "That would mean this particular piece was replaced."

"But why?" June asked. "What motive could the thief have?"

"Money is the top motive for most thefts, so we should start there." Maggie flipped to the next page of her notebook. "Since Ingrid and Craig were already stealing from the estate, they could have taken the pie safe to sell and left a reproduction in its place."

"Yes," June said. "Especially since Ingrid worked in the kitchen and could steer away anyone who looked too closely at the pie safe."

"And she'd also have access to the back door of the manor house to move large antiques without anyone seeing her," James added.

Maggie thought about Ingrid and Craig trying to make the exchange. "I can't see her or Craig waltzing down the street in the light of day with a big pie safe."

"The village isn't open every day, is it?"

"No," Maggie said. "But even on the days that it's closed, the caretaker is on the premises. They must have made the switch at night, which is possible since Ingrid had a key."

"So does Mr. Radcliff," James pointed out.

"Good point. As I get deeper into the mystery, I'm beginning to think he might be behind Amanda's abduction."

"Why, exactly?" James asked.

"He was the one who put the beehive in the kitchen," she

replied. "He said he didn't know about Ingrid's allergy, but don't you think that's odd? Sure, she kept to herself, but if you were severely allergic to bees, wouldn't you tell your employer in case anything happened? Especially if you were, say, a member of a historical reenactment village that featured a beekeeper?"

"Maybe she thought he wouldn't hire her to avoid a liability issue," James said. "I know it's illegal to discriminate, but that doesn't mean hiring managers don't do it all the time. And Mr. Radcliff could have sent the caretaker off-site for an errand, giving him time to bring in the replacement without anyone knowing about it."

"Makes him seem like a good fit for the theft, but what about abducting Amanda?" June asked. "Could he have done that, and if so, why?"

"If he did, he'd have had to put her somewhere close by that night, because we went to see him in his office around half past six, and he was there."

"If she disappeared as early as four, that would have given him plenty of time to hide her somewhere on the property," James said.

June swiveled toward Maggie. "What about the hidden stairwell? Might he have tied and gagged her, then stashed her in the stairwell until he had a chance to move her?"

Maggie pondered the idea, and a lightbulb came on in her head. "The stairwell entrance is in the kitchen, so maybe Ingrid saw him. That would explain why someone would want her dead." Thoughts of her own slow creep up the hidden stairs returned. "Oh, and there was sticky tape residue on the banister. I didn't pay it any attention, but if Amanda had been secured in there, it could be residue from duct tape. I'll give it another look as soon as we finish this discussion."

Maggie noted Mr. Radcliff's name on her pad and then added Craig's name too. "If Mr. Radcliff isn't guilty, maybe Amanda happened upon Craig taking money, and he abducted her."

"But then he would never let Amanda go, and the note on your pillow would make no sense at all. And why would he kill Ingrid?"

"It makes sense if it was meant to throw me off track and make me stop asking questions."

"Exactly," James said. "Just because it said that Amanda would be released doesn't mean that's the kidnapper's plan."

"But then who killed Ingrid, and why?" June asked. "Craig seems to be the only one around here who knew she was allergic to bees, but he doesn't appear to have a good reason to kill her."

James leaned forward. "What if we assumed they were behind the reproduction cabinet? Maybe they'd even switched out other items in the house. Ingrid and Craig could have had a falling-out over it, and he killed her."

"Ingrid did say that Amanda loved the primitive antiques, so I could see her paying close attention to them, and if she discovered they were fake, the Baldwins would have had motive to silence her too."

"My hands are always raw from polishing antiques." June rubbed her hands together. "If they worked with wood to make the reproductions, they'd have rough hands too."

"Ingrid's hands were red and chafed," Maggie said, "but that could come from working in the kitchen. I've shaken hands with Mr. Radcliff and his are baby-soft. Craig's, I'm not sure of."

"Then we need to check them out," James said. "I can go by the inn and shake hands with him."

"And I'll go check out the stairwell," Maggie said, "then talk to Mr. Radcliff."

June tapped her computer. "I'll keep looking to see if I can place a retail value on the pie safe."

"Do you have a ballpark guess?" Maggie asked her.

"Five grand or so."

James let out a low whistle. "For that price, the thief could have paid someone to make the reproduction, so we should also ask around about woodworkers in the area."

"Good idea," June said. "Though to keep from risking discovery of their thefts, the Baldwins probably wouldn't have used anyone in the immediate area."

"Good thinking, guys. I really appreciate your help." Maggie stood. "Okay, we all have our assignments, right?"

"One thing," James said. "Let's first walk through the house to look for other antiques that might have been changed out."

"Great idea," Maggie replied as she slipped on her coat. "I'll do that before talking with Mr. Radcliff so I have all the facts."

"I'm right behind you." James edged out of the booth seat and put on his jacket.

After Ingrid's death, Maggie didn't mind the company in the manor house and the stairwell, just in case. She grabbed Daisy's big flashlight from the counter and stepped outside.

She looked at the flashlight. "I'm not sure how I'm going to hide this from people as we stroll up Main Street."

James held out his hand. "My coat is kind of big. I can hide it underneath."

Maggie handed over the light and started up the street. "I'd love to come back here another time and really enjoy taking in the history—minus the hassle of wearing these clothes." She gazed enviously at him. "I don't suppose your attire is all that different from normal clothes."

"The shoes are terrible, and wearing a hat is annoying, but all in all it's not bad." He grinned. "At least I don't have to carry around thousands of pounds of fabric."

"While balancing in tiny shoes, I might add." Maggie cast her eyes from side to side as if looking for eavesdroppers, then leaned toward him. "Can you keep a secret?"

He raised an eyebrow.

She pulled up a bit of her skirt to show him her shoes. "June and I are cheating. We changed our shoes after church."

He laughed with her, and they walked on, enjoying each other's company as they made their way to the manor house.

Maggie climbed the stairs first, but he hurried ahead to open the door for her. She was eager to get to the stairwell, but she made a short detour to check out other antiques on the way. She stopped in the entryway to pick up another brochure for the house, and the stepback cabinet caught her eye.

She flipped through the brochure until she found the details for the antique. "This cabinet is by far the single most valuable piece in this house."

James walked over to the rope cordoning off the cabinet and ran a practiced eye over it. "Why is it so valuable?"

"It's made from yellow pine. Most of the yellow pine forests were depleted in the 1800s due to furniture making and export to Europe, so pieces like this one are rare and expensive."

"Expensive like the five grand June mentioned for the pie safe?"

She met his gaze. "More like twenty or thirty grand."

His eyes widened. "You're kidding, right?"

"You should know by now that I never kid about antiques." She wrinkled her nose at him.

He stared at the cabinet. "You don't think they would have risked changing out such a visible cabinet, do you?"

"It would take a lot of nerve." She looked around to see if anyone was watching, then opened the door to inspect the interior of the cabinet. "The answer is yes. The screws are wrong. This is a reproduction too."

"Man," James said. "Now we're talking about serious money."

"Let's hope it wasn't enough to drive someone to commit murder."

18

Maggie waited for a docent to step down the hallway with a small tour group, and then she slipped under the rope cordoning off the library. "We have to hurry before the guide returns."

"We definitely don't want to be caught sneaking around after what happened last night," James said.

Maggie glanced around the space for any obvious reproductions, but she was soon overwhelmed by the sheer quantity of antiques. "With the bookshelves, there are so many antiques in here that I don't know where to start."

"Let's assume that all of the ones taken were made of wood," James suggested. "The other items would be too hard to reproduce."

"Good point."

James inspected an early trade sign in the shape of a whale that was approximately three feet long and sitting on the fireplace mantel. Maggie found the item in the brochure, which declared it was cut from a single board of soft wood. It also claimed that the whale's teeth were made of handwrought nails.

Maggie took a closer look at the rusty nails. "The nails are square, which is fitting for the time period."

"So maybe it's an authentic antique."

She touched a nail. The rusty finish came off on her finger, revealing sleek metal underneath. "This isn't rust. The steel's newer, and it's been touched up to look old."

"Another reproduction, then."

"Looks like it." Maggie snapped a picture of the whale for June's research. "At least whoever faked this one knew enough to make the nails square."

"They're very visible," James pointed out. "And fake nails would be easier to spot, so they would have done the extra work to make it look real."

She moved to the bookshelves and lifted a wooden penny bank shaped like a miniature house with a highly pitched roof and topped with a carved rooster. Painted brown, the bank was carved to create a brick-and-mortar pattern. The bottom had an opening for retrieval of change, but it had been crudely bored, and the bottom of the piece was neither sanded nor painted brown to match the rest of the bank.

"The nails are wrong too," James said from directly behind her.

She jumped, nearly dropping the bank, but his arms came around her to rescue it. They stood for a moment, his arms wrapped around her, and she had to admit she liked how it felt to be so close to him.

She eased free. "Whoever made these items seemed to count on them not being picked up."

"I suppose people wouldn't dare when there are workers or volunteers around, but what about overnight guests?"

"Exactly." Maggie pondered the implication and set the bank on the shelf. "What if they didn't steal the items over time, but they were replaced all in one day, and the thief then planned to leave town with the originals?"

"Makes sense, but not for Craig and Ingrid. He seems determined to bilk as much money out of the estate as he can, and I think he'd hang around. The guy's got a strange sense of entitlement about this place."

"So Mr. Radcliff, then. If Amanda had caught him at it, he may have tried to take her out of the equation."

"Why wouldn't he replace the items at night when no one was around?"

She shrugged and sought a logical answer. "Maybe he had a

buyer for the items, and the deal had to be done during the day. Or this could have nothing to do with Amanda at all."

"True," James said. "I suppose we won't know until we find her."

Maggie snapped a picture of the bank with her phone, and they continued through the room, discovering a carved rabbit that had also been replaced. "We have a total of five items so far, and we've only looked in two rooms. The count is sure to go up when we do a more thorough search."

Maggie wanted to text the pictures to June, but it would have to wait until she had a signal on her phone.

"Time for the stairwell?" James asked.

Maggie led the way to the kitchen and the secret entrance to the stairs.

"If you hadn't seen Ingrid and Craig go in here, I doubt you would've discovered the stairwell."

"Agreed," she said and moved out of the way of the door as it swung open.

James turned on Daisy's flashlight and handed it to her. She shined the light at her feet and searched the floor for the tiniest scrap of evidence.

James turned on the flashlight app on his cell phone and pointed it above Maggie's head. "Do you really think Ingrid could overpower Amanda and get her up such steep stairs?"

"Sure, especially if Ingrid was armed."

"They didn't find a gun in her purse, but there are plenty of knives in the kitchen."

"Or she could have kept a gun on her person and her killer took it."

"True." James moved his light higher up the curving stairway. "There's a trail through the dust on these steps, as if something or someone had been dragged up them."

"And there are a ton of cracks and crevices where things could be hidden, so I'll be moving slowly." She searched each nook and cranny as she made her way up the first few steps. She continued until something shiny caught her eye.

She bent closer to see a silver Pac-Man earring. Her heart rate sped up. She took a tissue from her pocket, picked it up, and displayed it for James. "Lily said Amanda was wearing Pac-Man and Ghost earrings."

James looked up. "We should report this to Detective Adams."

"I agree. But not before I finish looking at the stairwell. It would probably be a good idea not to touch anything else as we look."

"Maybe we should back out of here now and not go any farther so we don't disturb evidence."

She gave his comment some thought. "I've already been in the stairwell, so my footprints and fingerprints are already here, but yours aren't. Why don't you wait at the bottom while I finish the search alone?"

He met her gaze and held it. "The door stays open so I know you're okay."

"Of course."

She climbed the creaking stairs, growing chilled in the drafty space. She paused in the spot where she'd seen the sticky residue. She leaned close, looked at it from the top, then sat and peered up at the underside.

"Aha," she said.

"What is it?" James called out.

"The sticky spot I felt before. There's a tiny strip of duct tape. It's looking more and more like Amanda was held here."

"Leave the tape in place for Detective Adams."

"I will," she replied, feeling a surge of appreciation for James's company and attention to detail. He always knew just what to do in difficult situations.

She continued higher, counting the stairs so she could tell Detective Adams exactly where to find the tape. She soon reached the top without discovering any additional clues.

She searched again on her way down and found a scrap of lace lodged in a brace holding the handrail. Maggie had seen a lacy handkerchief tucked into the wrist of Ingrid's gown the day they first met. She left it in place for the detective as well.

As she joined James, she turned off the flashlight and retrieved her notebook from her tote bag. She noted the stair numbers where she'd found the tape and the scrap of lace.

"There's lace stuck in the banister," she told James. "Ingrid had a lace handkerchief when I talked to her. It was tucked into her sleeve, so if it had already been snagged, I wouldn't have known. It could have happened if she fought with Amanda, or it could be from when she talked with Craig. All it proves is that she'd been in the stairwell, which we already knew."

James's eyes narrowed. "It's possible that Amanda discovered the stairwell on her own, right?"

"True," Maggie admitted. "But not as likely that she lost her earring without a scuffle."

"We should head over to the inn to see if Craig has rough and callused hands, and then report all of our findings to Detective Adams."

"You should visit Craig alone. If I'm with you, he might not be receptive to talking or shaking hands. I seem to rub him the wrong way."

"Good point."

"While you do that, I'll question Mr. Radcliff."

"Sounds like a plan."

They departed the house together and split up on Main Street. She found Mr. Radcliff seated behind his desk in his office.

"How can I help you, Ms. Watson?" He blew out a tired sigh.

"I wanted to ask you about the antiques in the manor house. The brochure says they're all original pieces."

"They certainly are. Every item in the house is from the Weatherly family's collection. We procured items for the other buildings over time."

"What would you say if I told you that some of the pieces are reproductions?"

He stood up tall and crossed his arms over his chest. "I'd ask what kind of scam you were trying to pull."

"So you know nothing about the pie safe and the stepback cupboard being replaced with reproductions, along with some of the pieces in the library?"

"That's preposterous. You must be mistaken."

"I'm not mistaken. We could go over to the house right now, and I'll show you how I know."

He grabbed his coat. "Let's go."

He stormed to the door and locked it after them. She had to jog to keep up with him as he marched across the clearing and up to the house. Inside, he stopped in front of the stepback cabinet and crossed his arms. "We have our antiques reappraised every few years for insurance purposes. They all checked out last year."

Maggie opened the cabinet door.

"Apparently, you don't pay attention to signs," he grumbled.

She ignored his protest and pointed inside. "Do you see these screws? Someone aged them to look old, but they were machine-made. Screws back then were handmade."

He took glasses from his pocket and put them on before bending close to the screws. "They're . . . oh my gosh." He met her gaze again. "But I don't understand. How . . . when . . . who—" He stopped and inhaled deeply. "It looks exactly like the original. I mean *exactly*, except for the screws."

"Yes, so whoever changed these out has to be skilled at woodworking or must know someone who is."

"Oh no. Oliver. What if it's Oliver?"

"Oliver, the caretaker?"

"Yes. He's a woodworker."

"I've visited his cottage. I didn't see any woodworking equipment."

"That's because he has a small cabin—shed, really—outside the village. The land is owned by the estate, but the trustees let him use the building for his cabinetmaking as a side business. They figure they're doing him a favor because they don't pay him much as caretaker."

"And he has time to do that along with caring for the village?"

"When the village is closed, he takes care of the estate property during the day and works on cabinets at night. He often reverses his schedule to keep away from the visitors when we have them."

Could he have been swapping out an antique the night she was stranded on the roof? He could have been the person skulking about, the one who left the picture in her room and faked a break-in to cover his tracks.

"I need to talk to Oliver about this, but he's doubtless at his cabin right now," Mr. Radcliff said. "I'll have to figure out a way to get out there. It's very remote, and at this time of year, the only way to reach it is by a snowmobile or snowshoes." He tapped his chin. "The sleigh is busy with guests, and I'm not about to snowshoe that far. I'll have to make other arrangements or wait for him to come back into town."

"What about contacting the police?"

"I will in due time, but I'd rather talk to Oliver first myself. If he's a thief, I'm sure I can get him to surrender himself at the station so as not to cause a scene here."

"But what if he has Amanda? We have no time to lose!"

"There's no proof that the theft is related to Amanda." He frowned. "And besides, I just can't see Oliver abducting a girl."

From what Maggie knew of the caretaker, she would agree, but she wasn't going to stake Amanda's life on her assumption. She had to figure out how to get to Oliver's cabin, and every minute could be costing Amanda far more than the value of a few missing antiques.

19

In the event that Oliver was at his cabin—which would mean Maggie had to don snowshoes—she quickly exchanged her dress for pants before jogging to Oliver's cottage. She pounded on the weatherworn door, but he didn't answer. Despite the curious looks from a crowd of tourists nearby, she peeked through his windows, but she didn't see him.

Fine. She was going on an adventure. She raced past the barn and livery until she reached the snowshoe rental hut. A memory of trying out an old pair of bear-paws that she'd found in the laundry room at Sedgwick Manor came rushing back. She'd been less than successful on that try, but fortunately, the snowshoes leaning against the hut were beavertail shoes, which she'd heard were easier for a novice to manage than bear-paws.

"One pair," she announced to the worker.

She handed him cash, and he took down a pair of snowshoes. She gave them a quick look. "These aren't antiques, are they?"

"No, but they are exact replicas of the shoes used in the 1800s by local villagers."

"Perfect." Maggie took the shoes and tried to imagine what life in this village must have been like after a big snowfall, with no snowplows to clear the streets or country roads. The snow roller would have helped a little, but it merely flattened the snow, and people still would have needed snowshoes to get around efficiently. She'd read once that even in the late 1800s, New York City didn't have anyone responsible for snow removal, and it had often fallen to the police to clear the streets. She found historical details like that fascinating.

She hugged the snowshoes to her chest and made her way to the livery to pay for a sleigh ride. As she handed over the cash, she thought of how such a simple thing as money could spur people like Craig and Ingrid to spend years committing crimes. She was glad her mind didn't work that way.

Loud bells jingled behind her, and she turned to see two large plow horses marching down the road. Maggie recognized the Hudson Valley sleigh that was used only by the wealthy elite of the day. The sleigh was black with burgundy leather seats and had a swan-body design that had been prevalent during the Victorian era. Maggie was sure sleighs like this could be valued at around $10,000.

The horses came to a stop and pawed at the ground with their large hooves while they snorted, their breath sending up clouds of vapor in the chilly air. The sleigh held four people and a driver. She counted four people ahead of her in line, but one was a toddler. Maybe the parents planned for the child to sit on one of their laps, which would mean there would be room for her on the next trip.

They boarded and the driver, a tall, gangly man wearing a long black coat, white breeches, and polished black boots turned to her. "Are you coming, ma'am?"

"I was waiting to see if there was room."

"They didn't buy a ticket for the kid." He eyed her snowshoes. "You won't need those on the ride."

She moved closer to him so the others wouldn't overhear. "Actually, I was hoping you'd drop me off as close to the caretaker's cabin as possible, and I'll snowshoe the remaining distance."

"Oliver's cabin?"

"Yes, do you know where it is?"

"Sure, but I saw Oliver in the village a few minutes ago. Why go all the way out there?"

"I want to see the architecture of the building." She blurted out the first thing that came to her mind.

"I don't know." He adjusted his tall top hat. "I'm not authorized to stop along the route and let visitors get off the sleigh."

"Mr. Radcliff has approved it." She didn't have his official approval, but she felt that stretching the truth a little might get her that much closer to finding Amanda.

He scratched his chin. "How are you planning to get back?"

"I can snowshoe back to the sleigh route and you can pick me up there."

"I usually have a full sleigh."

"Can I pay for tickets for several trips and then you can keep a spot open for me?"

He shrugged. "I suppose if you want to spend the money."

"I do. I'll pay now and be right back." She bolted toward the cashier before the driver could change his mind. She bought six tickets and gave them to the driver. "This should cover my return."

She set the snowshoes in the sleigh and climbed up. She settled in next to the mother holding the toddler and remembered taking Emily on a sleigh ride when she was about the same age. She had squealed and giggled, especially when the driver had let Emily pet the horses. Maggie thought she'd love it even now. Time had flown by so fast, and she could hardly believe Emily was in college. Maybe she could bring Emily here during her break next year, and then Maggie could spend more time enjoying the village with her daughter at her side.

The sleigh jerked and started forward. The metal runners glided smoothly over the snow, swooshing as they picked up speed and descended into an open field. The sleigh moved along at a brisk pace, and the only sounds were the runners swishing through the snow and the horses snorting as their hooves pounded over the field.

Before long, Maggie saw smoke rising from the chimney of a small cabin in the distance. The sleigh slowed, and she checked to be sure her phone had a signal. She wasn't foolish enough to get off the sleigh and go wandering around without a phone signal.

When the driver pulled the horses to a complete stop, she jumped down.

"Are you sure you'll be all right, ma'am?" he asked.

"I'll be fine, thank you," Maggie said, though she had no idea how well she'd do with the snowshoes. If she had real problems, she could call someone. If she were incapacitated in some way and couldn't return to this location, surely the driver would report her missing, as well as her intended destination.

She waved to her fellow riders as they drove off, and then she moved into the tracks from the sleigh to strap on her snowshoes. She set off on what appeared to be the shortest path to the cabin. She struggled with the first few steps, and she had to slow at times to navigate furrows in the field, but she developed a rhythm and soon neared the rustic log cabin with a single small window in the front.

A path leading to the rough-hewn front door had been pressed down by snowshoes. Maggie hadn't thought to ask how Oliver got woodworking supplies to the cabin in the winter. She supposed he used a sleigh or maybe a snowmobile to tow a trailer. She did remember seeing snowshoes and skis in his house, but at his age, would he snowshoe all the way? If he did, he certainly wouldn't carry supplies on his back.

Up close, she found a large metal hasp with a heavy padlock securing the door. She took that as a sign that Oliver wasn't here, and if Amanda was inside, Maggie could free her.

Maggie searched the space for another point of entry. The only other way in appeared to be the tiny window. She veered off the path and trudged to the window. The glass looked like it had been spray-painted black. *Odd.* Especially if Oliver didn't have anything to hide.

She leaned closer to the building.

"Amanda," she called out. "Are you in there?"

A groan sounded from the other side of the window. She thought of the photo of Amanda, bound and gagged, and she felt a sick feeling in the pit of her stomach. She looked around frantically for something to use to break the lock. She saw a large rock peeking through the snow and bent to pick it up, nearly face-planting in the snow when the weight of the rock caused her to overbalance.

After righting herself, she dug through the snow and slipped her fingers under the rock. Snow seeped into her mittens—the icy cold making her gasp—but she continued until she had the rock in her grip. She raised the rock and slammed it into the lock until the hasp broke and the lock fell to the snow. She heaved the rock to the side, then leaned over and shoved at the door. It swung open.

Sunlight filtered into the dark space. Directly ahead, Amanda sat in the same chair as in the picture, except now she was situated near a woodstove. Her mouth was covered with duct tape and her arms were tied to the chair. Her eyes were wide with fright.

Maggie's heart filled with relief, but she had no time to stop and enjoy the feeling.

"Hi, Amanda," she said gently as she popped off her snow-shoes. She slowly crossed the room, holding out her hands to show she meant no harm. "I'm Maggie Watson. I'm a friend of Lily's aunt Daisy, and I'm here to free you."

Amanda tried to speak through the tape but she was unintelligible. Maggie could guess what she meant by the tears filling her eyes at the sight of her rescuer.

"First, I need to call the sheriff's department." She dug out her phone. "I only have one pair of snowshoes, which will make getting us both back nearly impossible. The detective who's been looking for you will send help and we can get you out of here. Okay?"

Amanda started to nod, but then her eyes went wide, and she jutted out her chin in frantic motions as if she was trying to tell Maggie something.

"What is it?" Maggie asked.

Amanda jerked harder, thumped her hands on the chair, and tried to scoot the chair forward.

Maggie heard a noise behind her, and a shadow blotted out the patch of sunlight that had been streaming through the door around her. She turned to find the silhouette of a man standing in the doorway. She couldn't see his expression, but she could see all too clearly what he held in his hand.

It was a gun, and it was pointed right at her.

Panic assaulted Maggie. She glanced over her shoulder at Amanda. The fear in the young girl's eyes told Maggie she had to stay calm if they were both going to get out of this. Maggie took a deep breath, exhaled slowly, then forced a smile to her face.

"Hello, Oliver," she said as if she were greeting him in the village.

"You couldn't leave it alone, could you?" he snapped as he advanced into the room, his snowshoes still strapped to his feet. "Not even after I left you a picture and told you Amanda was fine."

"I didn't know if I could believe the person who left the note." *But if I had known it was you, I would have believed it, because I trusted you.* She almost kicked herself at the realization that she hadn't suspected him for a moment, when she'd suspected nearly everyone else she'd met at the village from the start.

"Looks like you chose not to, and now I have to deal with you too." He waved the gun at her, his eyes wild.

"Maybe you could tell me what this is all about, and perhaps we can come up with a solution."

"What this is *about?*" His voice rose and echoed through the cabin. "It's about the estate's board of directors reneging on their promises and cheating me out of my retirement—that's what it's about." The words flowed like venom from his mouth.

"What did they do?" she asked, making sure to keep her voice calm. "Help me understand, Oliver."

"They promised that after I worked at the village for ten years, they'd give me this cabin and the acre of land surrounding it. I planned to live here in my retirement, but no. The village has made a name for itself in the last five years and was showing a nice profit. So they decided to expand and use my cabin and land." He growled low in his throat. "Because of their promise, I've worked for a pittance all these years. I have no savings. I'm not going to go live on the street or in some home for paupers. I had to come up with a plan to get some money, and there was only one way to do it."

"The antiques," she said. "You replaced the most valuable ones with reproductions you've made."

"Pretty ingenious if I do say so myself, and I would have kept on doing it until there weren't any others I could reproduce. I'd have filled up my bank account so that when I couldn't work anymore, I could buy a little place of my own and live off social security."

"You had to know that someone would eventually discover the reproductions, and because you're a woodworker, they'd suspect you."

"Sure. But I didn't say I'd stay in the area. I planned to move south where it's warmer and disappear without a trace."

"And now?"

He jerked his gun at Amanda. "This little snoop saw me replacing a rabbit. I didn't think; I just snatched her right then and there."

"You put her in the stairwell in the manor."

"To buy some time to think. I suppose it would have been easiest to kill her then, but I'm not a killer." He eyed her, his gaze piercing. "At least . . . not yet."

"But you *are* a thief."

"They forced me to do all of this—don't you see?"

She didn't see how resorting to crime ever solved anything, but she kept that opinion to herself. "So what are your plans for Amanda?"

"I *had* planned that once the bank opened on Monday and I was able to liquidate my account, I'd scram and let the deputies know where to find her."

"But?"

"But that nosy old busybody, Ingrid, saw me grab Amanda," he said.

Maggie stifled her surprise. "Why didn't she report you?"

"I've known for some time that she and Craig were stealing money, and she discovered I was switching out the antiques. We both had our beefs with the estate, so we agreed to keep it between us and take as much as we could while we could."

"But she was worried that Amanda's disappearance would bring her thefts to light. So she asked you to let Amanda go. You couldn't do that, so you killed Ingrid."

"No! Her death was an accident." He took a deep breath and blew it out.

"But you did talk with her in the kitchen last night."

"You're right. She asked me to meet her. She'd followed me Thursday night when I moved Amanda from the stairwell. I thought everyone had left the village, and you people were all asleep in that tin can, so I took this girl to my car and drove her to an abandoned farmhouse down the road. Trouble was, Ingrid sat in her car and watched the main road with her headlights out and followed me. I led her right to Amanda." He shrugged. "But like I said, she was worried that both of our operations were compromised by the investigation into Amanda's disappearance, and she demanded that I release Amanda. I couldn't do that."

He raised the arm holding the gun, having let it drop to his side while he talked. "Ingrid got mad and grabbed the poker for the fireplace. She threatened me. I looked around for something to defend myself with and saw the beehive. I'd heard her talking with Craig once and knew she was allergic. I held out the hive figuring I'd scare her and stop her in her tracks."

"And then you broke it open to kill her."

"No! I only held onto it so I could get out of the kitchen and move Amanda again before Ingrid reported me and told them where I'd stashed the girl. If I moved her, she could be released on Tuesday like I'd planned. So I backed to the door, but the rug was all bunched up, and I slipped. As I reached out to stop myself from falling, I dropped the hive. It cracked open. The bees swarmed out. Ingrid panicked and started to run. I told her that honeybees weren't dangerous as long as she remained calm, but she kept waving her arms at the bees, upsetting them. They stung her like crazy."

He hung his head, and Maggie could see that he was truly grief-stricken over what had happened.

"I thought about calling 911, but she grabbed her EpiPen so I figured she'd be okay, and I had no time to waste. I had to move Amanda. I took off and brought the girl out here. I didn't know Ingrid died until this morning." His eyes glistened with tears, but he swiped them away angrily. "And now I have to figure out what to do with you."

"Tie me up until Tuesday too?" she suggested, grasping at straws. She had no intention of willingly letting him tie her up, but she wanted to keep him calm so he wouldn't take any more drastic action.

He smirked at her. "You're resourceful. I've seen that. Even admired it about you. But now . . . now I'll have to silence you. For good."

He's going to kill me.

Fear icing her nerves, she searched the room. There had to be a way out that she hadn't noticed yet.

He gestured with the gun at the corner holding a shelf. "There's duct tape on that shelf. Bring it and a chair over by Amanda."

She took slow steps toward the shelf. She heard Amanda squirming behind her and the muffled sounds of her attempts to say something. Maggie could tell from the look in her eyes that she thought Maggie would seal their fate if she let Oliver tie her up.

Maggie dredged up a comforting smile, then reached for the tape and noticed a pair of scissors sitting beside it. She thought to pick them up as a weapon, but Oliver would soon realize he needed them to cut the tape. No, she needed something she could hide in her jacket sleeve that he wouldn't notice was missing.

"What's taking so long?" Oliver snapped.

"Do you need the scissors too?" she asked meekly, all the while scanning her surroundings for another weapon.

"Yes, right. Bring them, but you better not try anything," he spat. "I will shoot you on the spot if I have to. Understand?"

"Perfectly." She put the scissors in the same hand as the tape. Then as she turned to walk away, she palmed a screwdriver in the other hand and slid it up her sleeve.

"Cut off two pieces of tape long enough to secure your wrists to the arms of the chair. Then drop the scissors on the floor."

She decided to obey, but she would take her time in doing so.

"Why don't you let us go now?" She grabbed the end of the sticky tape. "We promise not to tell anyone about your scheme." She peered at Amanda. "Right, Amanda? We won't tell anyone."

The teen frantically nodded.

"I can't trust that you won't." He waved his gun. "Now tape one of your wrists to the arm of the chair. Nice and tight now."

She ripped two strips of the tape free and did as he asked, securing the wrist without the screwdriver.

"Okay, good. Scissors on the floor now."

She set the scissors down between her chair and Amanda's so he'd have to bend down within reach.

"Nice try." He sneered. "Give it a good kick this way."

She held in a sigh of disappointment and used her toe to push the scissors closer to him.

"More," he said.

She gave the scissors a swift kick, and they spun across the floor, landing at his feet.

"Thank you." He stooped to retrieve them, keeping his eyes and gun trained on her.

He crossed the room. She slid the screwdriver down, making sure the metal part remained hidden behind her fingers. He kept his gun and his cautious gaze trained on her. He laid the second strip of tape over the top of her wrist, pressing it until it was fixed to her jacket sleeve.

Before he fully secured it, she took a deep breath and prepared herself to stab one hand and then knock the gun from the other one.

She paused. Despite all the damage he had done, she wasn't sure she could actually hurt this man. She swallowed hard. *But I have to get Amanda out of this.*

She counted down from five. *Four. Three. Two . . .*

The door burst open. Oliver jerked his head around. Maggie took her chance and jabbed at him, the blade of the screwdriver connecting with his gun hand. He howled in pain. The gun fell to the floor. Maggie kicked it away, sending it skittering across the floor to the far corner. He turned as if he were going to scramble after it.

"Hold it right there, Dorn!" James shouted as he came barreling into the room.

Oliver glanced around the space, then started to back toward the gun.

James launched himself at the caretaker. His arms wrapped around Oliver's midsection and the two crashed to the floor. James jerked Oliver's hands behind his back.

"Are the two of you okay?" James asked without looking up.

"I'm fine," Maggie said. "I want to get Amanda untied so we can ask her the same thing."

"I already called Detective Adams, and he's on his way."

"Good." Maggie came to her feet and dragged her chair across the room to grab the scissors. She cut the tape on her wrist and went to Amanda. "I'll free your wrists first so you can take the tape off your mouth yourself."

Tears continued to roll down Amanda's cheeks.

Maggie snipped the tape on her first wrist, and by the time she freed the second one, Amanda had ripped the tape from her mouth.

"Thank you, oh, thank you!" she cried.

"He didn't hurt you, did he?" Maggie squatted to slice through the tape on Amanda's legs.

"Not physically, no, but he scared me to death."

"I'm sorry you had to go through this," Maggie said and dug her phone from her pocket. "If you know your mother's cell number, we can call her to tell her you're okay."

"I don't know it. And besides, she's probably working." Her chin trembled and she bit her lip.

"Don't worry about it, honey," Maggie said, making sure her voice was soothing. "I have Daisy's number, and she can get ahold of your mother."

Maggie dialed and tapped her foot as she waited for Daisy to answer.

"I have someone here who is fine and wants to talk to her mother."

"Amanda?"

"Yes," Maggie said.

"Woo-hoo!" Daisy's boisterous shout came charging through the phone, and Maggie had to hold it away from her ear. "Let me get Suzanne on the phone, just a minute."

Maggie smiled at Amanda. "Daisy is getting your mother right now. She must have just arrived at the village."

Amanda's chin wobbled, and tears poured down her cheeks.

An excited voice suddenly came on the line. "This is Suzanne Caldwell. Is Amanda really there? Is she okay?" Her words came rushing out and tripped over each other.

"Yes, and she wants to talk to you."

"Thank God! Put her on."

Maggie passed the phone to Amanda, who could barely speak through her weeping. She managed to get out "Mommy?" before she broke down completely. Maggie could hear the voice on the other end of the phone breaking as well.

Maggie thought about what she would want someone to do for Emily if she were ever in such a horrific situation. She felt a strong urge to pull Amanda into a big hug, but that would have to wait until she finished her phone call. Comforting the girl in a smaller way didn't have to wait, though. Maggie squatted next to the teen and held her free hand.

After a few moments, Amanda seemed to recover herself a little, and a tremulous smile broke free on her tearstained face. "Mom wants to know how long before I get back to the village."

"It will be up to the detective," James said. "But I can hear a snowmobile in the distance, so I suspect it won't be long now."

Amanda relayed the information. "She wants to know if I can stay on the phone with her until she can see me."

Maggie squeezed Amanda's hand. "Absolutely."

Amanda returned to her conversation. Maggie wanted to ask James how he'd found them, but she didn't want to upset Amanda even more by dwelling on the ordeal. It was all behind them now.

Maggie could wait for the answer. They were safe and would soon be back at Weatherly Manor, in a beautiful historical village with their friends and family. For now, that was enough for Maggie.

21

Maggie climbed into the sleigh behind Amanda and put her arm around the shivering girl. She didn't know if the young woman was cold or still recovering from the terror of the last three days. Either way, Maggie knew Amanda needed the warm touch of someone who cared about her.

She had suggested that Amanda ride back on the snowmobile so she could be reunited with her mother faster, but Detective Adams said as long as he was on-scene, the snowmobile would remain in case of an emergency. She had to agree with him, though her mother's heart still balked.

James stepped into the sleigh and retrieved a heavy blanket from the other seat. He placed it over Maggie's and Amanda's legs. Amanda tugged it up tighter. He sat across from them, and Maggie wished he'd chosen to sit next to her. Not only for the warmth, but now that the incident was over and the shock of being held at gunpoint was settling in, she was trembling herself and longed for his reassuring presence.

The driver looked at them from his seat. "Are you all ready to go?"

"Yes, please," Amanda said through chattering teeth.

"Okay then, I'll get you to the village as fast as I can." He started the horses in a slow trot, then brought them to a swift canter.

Maggie lifted her gaze to James, and he smiled.

"Thank you," she mouthed.

His expression turned serious. Maggie understood the concern that lingered in his eyes. *What might have happened if he'd been too late?* She had to turn away from the intensity of his gaze to stare over the field. They soon merged with the normal sleigh route.

"I forgot my rental snowshoes at the cabin," she mused aloud.

"Mine are there too. I'm pretty sure we can arrange for Mr. Radcliff to have someone pick them up."

"You're probably right." She returned to watching the scenery pass by.

Amanda's stomach grumbled.

"Did Oliver feed you?" Maggie asked.

"Yes, but he stood over me with his gun, and I honestly didn't eat much."

"I know Daisy has a big lunch planned. Maybe you can eat something then."

"All I want to do is go home with my mom."

"I don't blame you," Maggie said, and she gave Amanda's shoulders a one-armed hug.

The village stop came into view, and Maggie smiled at the sight of a woman who was obviously Amanda's mother standing next to Jasmine and Lily, their arms wrapped around each other in a comforting embrace. Next to them, the women of the historical society and Mr. Radcliff waited and watched.

The moment the sleigh stopped, Suzanne rushed forward, and Amanda flung off the blanket to clamber over Maggie. She leapt into her mother's arms, nearly toppling them both.

Tears filled Maggie's eyes.

James came to sit next to her. "You did a good thing here, Maggie. I'm so proud of you."

"Even if you had to come to my rescue?"

"Somehow I think you would have gotten free without my assistance."

She believed the same thing. "How did you find me anyway?"

"When you didn't return from talking to Mr. Radcliff, June

got worried. She caught up with me at the inn, and we talked to Radcliff. He told us that Oliver was a woodworker and that you might have gone out to his cabin. June called Detective Adams, and I went to the sleigh. The driver confirmed that he dropped you off over an hour before. I grabbed some snowshoes and commandeered the sleigh. The rest you know."

"Thank you again." She took his hand and squeezed it quickly before climbing down out of the sleigh.

Suzanne let go of Amanda and grabbed Maggie in a hug. "Amanda told me what you did for her, and I will forever be grateful to you."

"No gratitude needed. I'm glad Amanda was found."

Suzanne pulled back. "Still, I'm thankful."

"Okay, everyone," Daisy said, her arm coming around Suzanne. "Let's get Amanda and Maggie out of the cold, and we can all have some lunch."

Amanda linked her arm with Suzanne's. "I just want to go home, Mom."

"Then that's what we'll do." Suzanne looked at Jasmine. "I'm so shook up. Could you drive us home?"

"I'd be happy to," Jasmine said and turned to her sister. "I know you're in charge of lunch. Maybe you can come over and pick me up after that."

"I can take care of getting lunch served," Ruth offered.

"It's not urgent," Jasmine said. "Lily can come with me, and I can spend some time with her too."

"You know, if I'm not there, lunch won't be served with my signature pizzazz," Daisy added with a wink. "And we have some celebrating to do!"

Everyone laughed, and they made their way up to the manor house. The moment the door opened, a spicy aroma hit Maggie's senses, and hunger pangs bit into her stomach.

"Chili, corn bread, and apple pie," Daisy said proudly. "I made them all this morning at the cute little diner in town. That Peggy is something for sure." Daisy put her hands on Maggie's shoulders. "You go have a seat in the dining room, and I'll bring both you and James a mug of hot cider."

"You don't have to wait on me," Maggie said.

Daisy waved her hand dismissively. "I finally figured out how to work the woodstove right, and I can't risk anyone else messing it up." She turned and started down the hallway, humming softly to herself.

"Well," James said and bowed with a flourish. "You heard Daisy, and we never argue with her."

Maggie chuckled and headed for the dining room, where she sat at the table with her friends, who peppered her with questions as Daisy served. The talk over lunch turned to the village and how they were all going to enjoy the last few hours together.

Maggie looked at James. "Maybe you'd like to go on a sleigh ride with me."

His brows lifted, but he grinned. "I'll go with you, Maggie Watson, but only if you promise that there won't be any surprises waiting for me at the end."

She grinned back. "With me, you never know."

To discover all that country decorating has to offer and see the creative home decorating tips that inspire Maggie and her friends, check out the latest issue of *Country Sampler* at CountrySampler.com!